GOLDEN DAWN

Also by Jenny Oldfield
published by Hodder Children's Books

Horses of Half-Moon Ranch 1: Wild Horses
Horses of Half-Moon Ranch 2: Rodeo Rocky
Horses of Half-Moon Ranch 3: Crazy Horse
Horses of Half-Moon Ranch 4: Johnny Mohawk
Horses of Half-Moon Ranch 5: Midnight Lady
Horses of Half-Moon Ranch 6: Third-Time Lucky
Horses of Half-Moon Ranch 7: Navaho Joe
Horses of Half-Moon Ranch 8: Hollywood Princess
Horses of Half-Moon Ranch 9: Danny Boy
Horses of Half-Moon Ranch 10: Little Vixen
Horses of Half-Moon Ranch 11: Gunsmoke

Home Farm Twins 1–20
Home Farm Twins Christmas Special:
Scruffy The Scamp
Home Farm Twins Summer Special:
Stanley The Troublemaker
Home Farm Twins Christmas Special:
Smoky The Mystery
Home Farm Twins Christmas Special:
Stalky The Mascot
Home Farm Twins Christmas Special:
Samantha The Snob
Home Farm Friends: Short Story Collection

Animal Alert 1–10
Animal Alert Summer Special: Heatwave
Animal Alert Christmas Special: Lost and Found

One for Sorrow
Two for Joy
Three for a Girl
Four for a Boy
Five for Silver
Six for Gold

GOLDEN DAWN

JENNY OLDFIELD

Illustrated by
Paul Hunt

a division of Hodder Headline

To Tammy Carroll and fellow dudes!

With thanks to Bob, Karen and Katie Foster, and to the staff and guests at Lost Valley Ranch, Deckers, Colorado

First published in Great Britain in 2000
by Hodder Children's Books

10 9 8 7 6 5 4 3 2 1

A Catalogue record for this book is available from the British Library

ISBN 0 340 75732 9

Typeset by Avon Dataset Ltd, Bidford-on-Avon, Warks

Printed and bound in Great Britain by
The Guernsey Press Co. Ltd, Channel Isles

Hodder Children's Books
a division of Hodder Headline
338 Euston Road
London NW1 3BH

1

'Horses are the dumbest thing on earth!' Red Lockhart muttered. He cursed under his breath as the broodmare, Golden Dawn, moved right in front of Tatum, her two month old foal, and prevented him from taking the perfect picture.

'Yeah, the dumbest thing except for photographers!' Lisa Goodman murmured.

Kirstie Scott grinned. 'What's so stupid about Golden Dawn trying to protect her foal?' she asked the irritable cameraman.

'Because I only plan to take a photograph, not

shoot her down with a gun!' he grumbled. 'Listen; I just had to get out of bed at four a.m. and drive thirty miles to be here at Half-Moon Ranch by dawn.

'I'm set up in the meadow as the sun gets up, my feet are freezing, my belly's so empty it sounds like the insides of an old steam boiler, and what does the stupid animal do? It gets between me and the moment. All I have is a giant nostril and half an ear, looming up in front of my lens!'

'Huh!' Matt Scott, Kirstie's older brother, was showing his exasperation too as he strode across the frosty grass. He took hold of Tatum's leather headcollar to stop the tiny sorrel foal from straying further out of shot.

'Horses aren't dumb. It's the people around 'em!' Kirstie whispered to Lisa. She stood, arms folded, watching the two men trying to line mother and foal up for another photo opportunity. Meanwhile, a golden-red sun peeked over the top of the Meltwater Mountains, and a pink light began to wash down the slopes towards Red Fox Meadow.

Lisa giggled. 'Is that "people", period? Or some people in particular?'

'That's "guys" in general,' Kirstie confirmed.

The two girls noted Golden Dawn pushing her soft brown nose up against Red's camera lens while the photographer fought her off in vain. In the background, Matt slipped and slid over the ice at the edge of Five Mile Creek as little Tatum showed surprising strength in dragging him across the meadow.

'Hah!' Lisa couldn't help grinning as the thin ice cracked and Matt's heeled cowboy boot disappeared into six inches of crystal clear running water.

'Time to step in!' Kirstie decided, glancing up at the rising sun and tucking her long fair hair down the collar of her padded vest. Then, delving deep into her pockets, she strode forward. 'Where d'you want the horses to stand?' she asked Red politely.

He emerged frowning from the headbutting he'd just received from a protective and wary Golden Dawn. The mare was a beautiful rich sorrel, darker than her foal, but with the same bright white star on her forehead. 'In an ideal world, I'd like them two paces in from the bank of the creek, both heads turned towards the camera.'

'Some hope!' Matt grunted as he finally let go of Tatum's headcollar and stooped to take off his wet boot. 'Whose idea was it to take dawn shots for our new brochure anyhow?'

'Yours!' Lisa and Kirstie fired back at him. Matt had been the one who'd decided to update the ranch's publicity. Red Lockhart was a fellow student at the Denver college where Matt studied veterinary science, and Matt had convinced his mom, ranch owner Sandy Scott, that his buddy would take great shots to show Half-Moon Ranch in its best possible light.

That had been the theory. But the practice this spring Saturday morning was proving somewhat more complex.

'How would it be if I could get Goldie and Tatum to pose right here?' Kirstie suggested with a smile hovering at the corners of her wide mouth.

'Yeah, right; you and the US cavalry!' Red scoffed as he cleaned his camera lens with a scrap of soft fabric.

Kirstie ignored him and clicked her tongue gently against the roof of her mouth to attract the mare's attention. Wherever Golden Dawn went, Tatum would be bound to follow.

'Here, Goldie. Here, girl!' she murmured, one hand still dipped deep into her pocket.

The sturdy sorrel mare twitched her nostrils and pricked her silky ears. Steadily she stepped across to the spot chosen by Kirstie for that special Kodak moment, her heavy hooves crunching into the frozen turf, head nodding gently as she approached.

Red raised his camera and looked through the viewfinder. 'Yeah, that would be great. The sunlight is just catching the tops of those ponderosa pines behind the ranch house. It looks like they're on fire! Hey, Matt, get out of shot, will ya?'

Still Golden Dawn made a steady beeline for Kirstie. Tatum too had begun to totter towards the desired spot as Kirstie's brother snuck off to one side.

'Yeah, breakfast!' Kirstie whispered, taking her hand from her pocket and offering the mare a fistful of grain pellets.

Golden Dawn stretched out her neck and snatched the feed with her rubbery lips. She chomped on the pellets, grinding them noisily between her back teeth.

Red stood, camera poised.

'Hold it. Here comes Tatum!' Lisa breathed.

The foal was all head, legs and skinny ribs. His tufty mane was soft as cotton wool, his tail a stumpy feather-duster swishing behind. And his liquid brown eyes were big as saucers as he skipped up alongside his mom.

'Take your time. Here's dessert!' Softly Kirstie stroked the mare's nose before handing over a second generous helping of pellets. She felt the mare's lips suck up the feed, waited one more second, then stepped smoothly out of camera shot.

Click! The photographer seized the moment.

Sorrel mare and foal looking directly at camera. Eyes big and shining. Behind them a crystal creek. Behind that a log ranch house backed by flame-tipped trees. And the golden sun on the horizon, lighting up the rugged peaks, turning the quiet grey landscape pink, waking up the blue jays, introducing a new day.

'How about an action shot?' Red suggested next. He was happy with the mother and foal pose and was moving on. 'We could get a great picture of the whole herd of horses running free along the Jeep road over there!'

'Hmm.' This time, Kirstie wasn't so sure. To organise thirty-plus quarter-horses all moving in the same direction at a gallop was a pretty tall order.

'That'd take a whole truck-load of grain pellets, I guess,' Lisa shrugged.

'Sure.' Noticing that Matt had sloped off back to the house and left them to complete the photographic assignment without him, Kirstie tried to explain to the city boy. 'Horses are smart, OK?'

With a slow nod, Red acknowledged the truth of this.

'But they only act that way if they can see it's to their advantage. So, like, what's the point of them all crowding up on to the Jeep road and setting off at a gallop for no reason? They wouldn't get it, see?'

Red tipped back the peak of his baseball cap to scratch his tousled fair head. 'Yeah, gotcha.'

Lisa too joined in the discussion. 'Like, we know that in terms of IQ, horses are rated way down there just above sea anemones and squid.

Their brains are wired different to ours . . .'

'Yeah, yeah, cut the physiology lesson,' Red interrupted, glancing at his wristwatch. He turned back to Kirstie. 'Just tell me how we get a head-on shot of the whole gang thundering down the track.'

She thought hard. 'Food!' she said at last. 'That's always the bottom line. C'mon, Lisa, help me load up the truck with alfalfa. We'll work out a strategy, assume positions, ask Charlie to open the meadow gate, then stand by and watch!'

'Sure we will . . . !' Lisa screwed her face into a doubtful frown.

But Red backed Kirstie. 'Let's do it!' he cried impatiently, camera at the ready.

'All set?' The young wrangler, Charlie Miller, stood at the meadow gate and radioed to Kirstie and Lisa, who sat in the pick-up with three bales of hay. Between them lay a half mile stretch of dirt track running alongside Five Mile Creek.

Lisa checked Red Lockhart's position in the forked trunk of a tall pine tree. He sat poised, pointing his camera down the empy track, so she nodded at Kirstie.

'Kirstie to Charlie. We're ready to roll! Over.'

'Charlie to Kirstie. You sure this is gonna work? Over.' Evidently the young wrangler, who had been roped in to help along with Matt, shared Lisa's original doubts.

'Kirstie here. Let's go through it one more time. Number one: you already split off the mares and foals from the main ramuda? Over.'

'You bet. Over.'

'Number two: the rest of the horses are bunched up by the meadow gate, right? Over.'

'They're rarin' to go. Hollywood Princess and Johnny Mohawk are right up front. Over.'

'And Matt's at the wheel here, ready with a bait of alfalfa. As soon as the horses hit the track, we start driving slowly towards the bottom meadow. Hollywood and Johnny spot food and chase after us. We catch them all safe and sound by the pond. What can possibly go wrong? Over.'

There was a pause, then Charlie's crackly voice came faintly through. 'Did you check this with your mom? Over.'

'Mom already drove to town with Ben. Over.' The head wrangler had set off early with Sandy to visit a sale barn in San Luis. 'Let's do this, shall we? Red's so excited he's practically falling out of his tree. He seems to be shouting something about the light being right. Over.'

'OK, you're the boss!' Charlie clicked off his radio and swung open the meadow gate.

'All this for a dumb brochure!' Lisa muttered. She braced herself as Kirstie leaned sideways and gave the signal for Matt to ease forward with the truck-load of hay.

They crawled down the Jeep track, aware of the jostle of horses at the gate. Kirstie easily spotted the pure white form of Hollywood Princess leading the bunch. The stunning horse half reared, then swerved in the direction of the hay-laden pick-up. She thundered towards them, with athletic Johnny Mohawk close on her heels.

'Faster!' Kirstie yelled at Matt. At this rate, the herd would outrun the truck before they reached the safety of the second meadow.

Her brother picked up speed and jerked her and Lisa back against the bed of sweet-smelling hay. Up in his tree, Red perched and waited.

'Wow!' Picking herself up, Lisa peered over the tailboard. She saw the dust raised by stampeding hooves, the flick of manes and tails, a solid sea of loping backs – white, black, brown and spotted – all heading their way and gaining on them.

Lucky, Crazy Horse, Jitterbug, Rodeo Rocky – Kirstie picked them out one by one. Her own palomino would be in the picture if he stayed where he was, tucked close in behind Johnny Mohawk. That's if you could see a horse at all for the dust they were raising!

'What the heck . . . ?' Hadley Crane's voice rose above the drum-roll of galloping hooves. The old wrangler had just emerged from his cabin on the hill and come face to face with a mass of what looked like escaping steeds.

Despite his seventy years, he sprinted downhill like a youngster to cut the horses off.

'No, Hadley; wait!' Lisa yelled.

Too late. The old man cried out and waved both arms at Hollywood, diverting the leader of the herd from her planned route along the Jeep track.

Red looked down to see what had happened and almost fell out of his tree. The jittery horses suddenly lost interest in their alfalfa breakfast, and swerved up the hill along Brown Bear Trail, heading straight for the main exit from the ranch.

'Oh, great!' Kirstie felt her stomach twist and

flip. Out beyond the gate of Half-Moon Ranch was a mountainous wilderness of National Forest territory stretching mile after mile towards Eagle's Peak. Worse still, between the herd of horses and their unexpected bid for freedom lay a treacherous and deep cattle guard.

She pictured sweating horses reaching the grille, imagined the scared jostling for position between say Navaho Joe and Cadillac. They would knock into each other as they approached the wide obstacle, throw each other off balance. Some would fail to take the cattle guard in their stride. There would be broken legs; horses would have to be destroyed . . .

'Drive!' Kirstie yelled at Matt. 'We have to open the gate, let them through. C'mon, move it!'

He drove. Foot squeezed hard to the floor, the engine roared and the truck crunched gravel as it flew up the hill only yards ahead of the horses.

'Faster!' Lisa cried, hanging on to the side of the truck.

They gained a little ground, gave themselves maybe ten seconds to open the gate next to the cattle guard. Not enough time to turn the herd and head it back towards the ranch; just enough to create a safe exit out into the forest.

Kirstie dived from the truck before it had fully stopped, then unlatched the iron gate. She and Lisa swung it open. Hollywood swerved for the space and sped by at a bruising speed, hooves thumping the dirt, white mane flying. Johnny Mohawk came a close second, then Lucky, then Jitterbug, then a blur of pounding, jostling shapes.

'Huuh!' Kirstie let out a sigh of relief, aware of Hadley, Red and Charlie labouring on foot up the steep hill after the fleeing horses. 'At least no one broke a leg in the cattle guard!'

Silence. The sound of hooves grew duller. And Half-Moon horses disappeared out of sight in a cloud of dust.

'Lisa?' Slowly Kirstie turned to face her friend.

'. . . Kirstie!' A croak escaped from between Lisa's clenched teeth. She pointed with a trembling finger to Matt standing helpless at the edge of the cattle guard.

No; not at Matt, but at the pick-up parked on the slope behind him. Well, not parked exactly.

In his panic over the horses, Kirstie's brother must have jumped out of the cab without applying the handbrake. And now the truck was easing backwards, slowly at first, then gathering speed – *bump, rattle, bump* – in reverse towards a granite boulder the shape of a giant sugar lump!

'O-o-o-ohhh!' Kirstie only dared look through the cracks between her fingers as she raised both hands to her face.

The empty pick-up rocked and rolled down the uneven slope. *Scrape, scratch, knock-knock!* It bounced from boulder to boulder, scattering alfalfa, ricocheting between the trunks of trees until it finally hit the sugar lump.

Crunch!

Silence again.

Sunlight dappled through the trees on to the wrecked truck, its back fender crumpled unrecognisably, pale green hay spread on the forest floor like confetti.

'And I didn't even get my action shot!' Red Lockhart wailed as he arrived on the spot, breathless and minus his camera.

Hadley had got there before him and was staring down the empty road. 'Forget action shots,' he muttered grimly, hands on hips, the brim of his stetson shadowing his thin, lined face.

'Dang me if you ain't just gone and lost every available mount on the whole darned ranch!'

2

'Yeah, we did act pretty dumb!' Kirstie admitted. Though she didn't show it, she felt seriously worried by the escape.

It was midday Saturday. Sandy Scott and Ben were back from the sale barn without having lit upon any likely new candidates to join the Half-Moon Ranch ramuda.

Which meant that Hadley's statement still held good; the dude ranch was without a single serviceable quarter-horse for incoming guests to ride.

Standing at the main gate, frowning deeply at the wrecked pick-up, the ranch boss considered what to do.

'Which way did the horses head after they stampeded through the gate?' she asked Matt quietly.

'They went north towards Aspen Park. I guess you didn't see any signs of them when you were driving home?'

'Nope.' Sandy gazed down the hillside towards the empty meadow. 'Where are the mares and foals?'

'They're in Pond Meadow,' Kirstie assured her. 'Charlie cut 'em out and made sure they were secure down there before he opened the gate to let the rest run free. We didn't want the foals getting trampled in the rush.'

Sandy sighed. 'Thank the Lord for small mercies.' Then she turned to Ben, her head wrangler. 'How about we peek our heads up around Aspen Park?' she suggested.

He nodded. 'We'd need to trailer the three broodmares out with us. We'll use them to round up the escapees.'

It was Kirstie's turn to frown. 'Uh-oh. The foals

have never been separated from their moms before,' she whispered anxiously to Lisa. Golden Dawn, Taco and Yukon had all foaled within the last three months and the youngsters were scarcely weaned. But she did realise that Ben's plan was the only viable one, and even then it might prove difficult for three riders to round up more than thirty horses currently enjoying their new-found freedom in the vicinity of Aspen Park.

'OK, so long as we get them back to their foals by dusk,' Sandy decided, sending Ben and Charlie to organise the tack and the trailer.

'Mom, I'm real sorry about this,' Matt began. He was left to carry the can after his friend, Red, had made a hasty exit before Sandy and Ben arrived back at the ranch.

'Sorry doesn't quite do it, son,' she replied with a shake of her head. 'Listen, I'd like you to take care of the truck while Ben and I go look for horses.'

Matt didn't argue. He looked crestfallen and hung his handsome head, kicking at the dirt with the toe of his boot.

'Can I come along?' Kirstie asked. She too was

feeling seriously guilty. She knew they were expecting an influx of guests next day: twenty-three to be exact. And each one was looking to ride out and round up cows during Spring Cattle Week. 'How about I ride Golden Dawn?'

Sandy nodded OK without speaking, while Matt stumbled downhill towards the beat-up trailer.

'What about me?' Lisa hissed. 'I don't want to miss out on the action!'

'Why not come along for the drive? We could use an extra pair of hands to load horses into the trailer when we catch 'em.' Kirstie was forcing herself to look on the bright side, thinking that they would soon track down the fugitives and entice them back home.

And this was how the plan turned out; Matt, Hadley and Charlie were left to clear things up at the ranch, while Sandy, Ben, Kirstie and Lisa set out with the three mares loaded into the trailer in the early afternoon.

'Leave the alfalfa where it is,' Sandy instructed Charlie, who had come up the hill to the main gate with a rake to gather up the spilled feed. Her mind was buzzing with details of what needed to be done in her absence. 'The deer and the cows will enjoy the treat. Oh, and Hadley, could you call Chuck Perry and check that he shows up here first thing Monday? We have a couple of horses who've thrown shoes in the past week.

'And then call the engineer over at Dorfmann Lake, see if they plan to open up the dam and let out overspill into Five Mile Creek. If they do, we need to move the foals out of Pond Meadow just in case of a flash flood.'

'Yes, ma'am,' the old man said briskly. He went straight off to perform the tasks he'd been given.

'Oh, and Matt . . .' Sandy paused before climbing up into the trailer cab to join Ben and the girls. She managed a smile and a forgiving shrug. 'Hey, it's not the end of the world!'

Sheepishly he grinned back. 'Next time, I'll set things up better,' he promised.

'Don't even *think* about a next time!' his mom said quickly. She climbed into the cab then leaned out of the window. 'From now on, as far as pictures for the brochure are concerned, we stick strictly to shots of cosy cabin interiors, sweet mothers and foals; all that easy stuff!'

* * *

In spite of everything, Kirstie enjoyed the drive out.

The road from the ranch took them through densely pine-forested slopes towards the main route into San Luis. But after a couple of miles of uneven dirt track, Ben took a left turn, following a hand-painted wooden sign towards Aspen Park. It took them out of the canopy of trees into broad sunlight and a rolling stretch of scrubland scattered with thorn bushes. Tall spears of yellow-flowering Indian tobacco plants rose from fleshy green leaves, while clumps of paintbrush cacti splashed vermilion against the yellowish earth.

While Kirstie and Lisa enjoyed the space and the fresh spring colours, Sandy and Ben concentrated on looking for tracks.

'Those horses sure churned up the ground,' Ben commented, pointing out how easy their trail was to follow. It seemed that the first guess had been right; Hollywood and co had continued to head north towards the green pastures of Aspen Park.

The park lay three or four miles down the track from the turn-off, beyond the dome-shaped scrubland, through more ponderosa pines and continuing on up a steady incline towards a patch of vivid green aspen trees. In a sheltered hollow behind the stand of trees was the grassland area belonging to neighbouring rancher, Waddie Newton.

'How come the horses knew where to head for the best grass around?' Lisa queried. She sat sideways in a space behind the driver's seat, her legs hunched up to her chest, face to face with Kirstie, who was also squeezed into the same narrow space.

'Some of them, including Hollywood, just spent the winter months up here,' she explained. 'You get good grazing all year round, and Waddie rents the land out to us. He splits it between our horses and Jim Mullins' cows, though I heard a rumour recently that he plans to sell it on to a developer up in Denver.'

'Over my dead body!' Sandy insisted from the front of the cab.

'You mean, they want to build *houses*?' Lisa gasped, gazing out at the beautiful hillside.

Sandy glanced round. 'Like I said, over my dead–' She stopped suddenly as Ben slammed on the brakes.

'Mule deer!' he warned, bringing the trailer to a crunching halt.

Kirstie saw that they had stopped twenty or thirty yards short of half a dozen of the graceful, slender creatures. The deer stood sideways on and immobile on the track; a doe, two fawns and three yearlings. The doe twitched her large ears, head raised and turned nervously towards the noisy, fume-spreading vehicle. She'd shed her grey winter coat and shone a healthy reddish brown in the sun. Her throat was white, her short tail tipped with black.

'I so wish I could take their picture!' Lisa breathed.

'Please, no more cameras!' Sandy whispered back. 'Not today, anyhow!'

They all smiled and waited for the small group of deer to move on. The doe continued to stare at the trailer with her huge dark eyes, while, partly reassured, the yearlings dropped their heads to nibble at the roadside grass. The fawns meanwhile stuck close to their mother, wobbling unsteadily on their stick-like legs.

'Why don't they carry on over the ridge?'

Kirstie was puzzled by the deer's reluctance to proceed.

'There must be something they don't like over there, I guess.' Ben reckoned he had the answer and was prepared to let the engine idle until they found out if he was right.

Sure enough, the doe turned her attention away from the trailer and looked up the ridge towards a moss-covered boulder surrounded by a clump of prickly thorn bushes. Staring hard, Kirstie thought she made out a small movement there.

'Coyote!' Ben guessed again.

'Whatever – she sure don't like the look of it.' Lisa's gaze was glued to the bush now, so she jumped in surprise when the deer turned in their tracks and bounded back the way they'd come.

Led by the doe, with the fawns bunched close behind, and the yearlings bringing up the rear, they jumped and loped over the rough ground, gathering speed and hardly pausing to clear the four foot wire fence that marked the southern boundary of Aspen Park.

'Yep, coyote,' Sandy confirmed. As the deer vanished into some leafy aspens, she pointed out more movement from the thorn bushes.

A silent shape crept out, and began to skirt around their trailer at a distance of forty yards. The creature looked and behaved like a fox, except that he was twice as big and his long, thick coat was a flecked grey and white. His snout was long and pointed; his bushy tail brushed the ground as he padded by.

'Uugh!' Lisa shivered.

Untroubled by their presence, only perhaps angry that they'd helped reveal his presence to the unsuspecting deer, the coyote gave them a cold stare with his glaring, yellow eyes.

'Let's go!' Kirstie urged. A coyote, like a mountain lion, was one creature she'd always rather avoid. Bears; no problem. You just stood your ground, looked big and eyeballed them into backing off. But coyotes were scavengers capable of bringing down a young deer if they hunted in packs. And she hated the fierce, glassy look in their glowing, confidence-shattering eyes.

Giving the eerie predator time to break into a smooth trot and disappear into another thicket of thorn bushes, Ben at last eased the trailer forward. Now nothing lay between them and the entrance into Aspen Park except another half mile of churned-up track which the fleeing horses had recently passed along.

The wrangler drove the last stretch and pulled up under a row of silver-barked aspens by a roughly made wire gate.

'Looks like the horses took a run at it and didn't care too much about making a clean jump,' Lisa commented, pointing out the twisted and trampled strands of wire as evidence of what she'd said.

Kirstie winced as she pictured Hollywood, Johnny and probably Lucky and a couple of others making a neat clearance, followed by a ragged troop of short-legged horses such as Crazy Horse, Squeaky and Chigger. Eager to get at the lush grass inside the park and not get left behind, they would most likely have risked cutting themselves to ribbons on the razor-wire.

'C'mon, let's saddle up those three mares and get out there after them,' Ben said swiftly. He took Taco, the first horse to be led out of the trailer. Then Sandy went in for Yukon, the brown-and-white paint. A sensible, plodding type of animal, Yukon would nevertheless do her very best to help them round up the herd.

Kirstie stroked Yukon's nose as she came down the ramp, then slipped inside the trailer to untether Golden Dawn. The sorrel greeted her with an impatient shove of the head, as if to say, 'Get a move on and get me outta here! If there's a job you want me to do, let's do it!' She stamped across the metal floor and down the ramp, sniffing at the air, then raising her head to whinny loudly.

There was nothing sensible or plodding about Goldie, Kirstie knew. Like many sorrel mares, she was highly-strung, even a little bad-tempered, especially when someone came between her and her precious Tatum. So she shifted restlessly while Kirstie put on her saddle blanket and then her heavy, horned saddle, prancing when her cinch was tightened, tossing her head and refusing to open her mouth when the bridle was offered.

'Oh, c'mon, girl!' Kirstie muttered. 'Don't kid me you suddenly turned bit-sour!' Gently she eased her thumb into the corner of the horse's mouth until Golden Dawn relented. Soon the bridle was buckled and they were ready to go.

From her vantage point inside the cab, Lisa had been scanning the pasture beyond the park entrance while the others tacked up. Now she leaned out and hissed the word, 'Horses!' into Kirstie's ear.

'Where?' Fresh in the saddle, Kirstie reined Golden Dawn to the right and peered up the hill.

Making herself as useful as possible, Lisa leaped down from the trailer and ran to open the trampled wire gate. 'Past that broke-down cabin, under the aspens!'

Kirstie spotted the place and nodded. She checked with her mom and Ben, then together they set off at a slow lope.

'Easy, girl!' Kirstie murmured to Golden Dawn. She felt the surge of power as the strong mare tried to break into a full gallop. But she knew they had to approach the creatures under the trees with caution; Aspen Park covered a whole heap of territory and there were many square miles for the ranch horses to flee through.

'Don't spook them!' Ben muttered an unnecessary warning. He too was having a hard time holding Taco back as the sturdy quarter-horse set her mind on covering ground fast. Her solid hindquarters bunched and she got ready to power forward past the derelict cabin. 'Easy, girl!'

Ben echoed Kirstie and tightened the reins.

'Uh-oh!' Sandy sat back further in Yukon's saddle as she saw first one horse, then another lift its head at their approach. The escapees knew they were here.

Kirstie recognised the brown spotted coat of Navaho Joe and the distinctive light tan coat and pale mane of ugly old Crazy Horse. These two horses were nearest to the approaching riders, and as they snickered, four or five others left off grazing and bunched closer together.

'Looks like they're gonna give us a hard time,' Ben muttered. 'They've all split into small groups and no way are they gonna put up their hands and surrender!'

No sooner said than Navaho Joe, the free spirit of the Half-Moon Ranch ramuda, split off towards the hilltop. The Appaloosa reared and turned, streaking away from them with his long white tail streaming behind him. Close on his heels went Crazy Horse, then Silver Flash, followed by Kirstie's very own palomino, Lucky.

'OK; you want a race, you got it!' Kirstie muttered, digging her heels into Golden Dawn's sides.

The sorrel mare took off at a gallop, surprising her rider with her sudden burst of speed. But then, the mare was fresh, not tired after a ten mile sprint like the rest of the horses. And besides, she had Tatum to get back to.

So she flew by the deserted, crumbling cabin, past its rusted iron cooking-range and collapsed dog kennel. She jumped clear over the felled pine trees which the logger owners of the cabin had left behind to decay back into the earth. And she ate up the ground towards the ridge, swerving between aspens, breathing hard as she gained on Joe and the rest.

'Now I know why cowboys need lassos!' Kirstie muttered, a picture in her mind of raising the rope above her head, circling it, then letting it fly at the fleeing horse in front of her. But seriously, she was glad to avoid the sight of the harsh rope digging into flesh, leaving a burn mark where it had tightened hard round the horse's neck.

No; the trick was to work a pincer movement between her and her mom on Yukon, with Ben and Taco bringing up the rear. They would run Joe and the rest up against a fence, corner them and gradually turn them back towards the gate.

With luck, Lisa would be waiting there with the trailer door open and space for the first four runaways.

Which was exactly how it happened.

There was a glorious chase through lush pasture; a log to jump here, a tree to swerve around there. Kirstie felt the wind in her hair and the solid, rhythmical gallop of Golden Dawn beneath her.

Catch me if you can! The look in Joe's eye had contained high spirits and a sense of adventure. His easy gallop had expressed grace, the toss of his head a suggestion that this was all a pleasant game.

'Like, we really want to play tag with you!' Kirstie sighed, digging in for the chase. She settled her butt into the deep saddle and urged her horse on, aware that the pincer tactic would take effect any minute.

'Whoa!' Ben cried. The runaway horses had come up against a boundary fence and ground to a halt. First Joe, then Lucky, Silver Flash and Crazy Horse dug in their heels just in time.

'Hah, gotcha!' Kirstie cried, pulling Golden Dawn up short. Her horse was breathing hard, her shoulders sweating and lathering up. But they'd succeeded in cornering four of the fugitives.

Then six more, then three, and so on through the afternoon. As soon as the trailer was full, Ben handed over Taco to Lisa and drove the recaptured horses back to the ranch. Kirstie, Sandy and Lisa were to carry on with the round-up while he was gone.

'Three trips should do it,' Sandy predicted as the loaded trailer departed for the first time. 'That's if all the horses made it as far as the park.'

'Sure they did. The herd would stick together, whatever happened.' Kirstie knew the habits of horses; there was safety in numbers for them, and she was certain that all would be found.

'Twenty-nine, thirty, thirty-one!' Lisa counted as the last runaways trudged up the ramp.

It was twenty after five; a full, saddle-weary three hours of rounding up reluctant ranch horses later.

'Twenty-eight, twenty-nine, thirty!' Kirstie contradicted with a frown.

Inside the trailer, two horses – Johnny

and Jitterbug – rocked the boat.

'Thirty!' Sandy confirmed, then double-checked with Ben.

'Thirty. That still leaves one missing,' he reminded them.

Kirstie ran through the list of recaptured horses one more time. 'Guess who!'

'Don't tell me . . . Hollywood!' Lisa's answer was prompt. She too had missed the gorgeous, glamorous pure white horse. 'Wouldn't you just know it!'

Hollywood Princess was the prima donna of the herd. Along with her stunning good looks, a dynamic mixture of vanity and smartness cut her out from the crowd, and it was no surprise to anyone that she was the last horse to be brought in from the park.

'Even Hollywood won't want to stay out alone all night,' Sandy predicted, sagging in her saddle, yet ready to cowboy up for one last effort. 'C'mon, let's go find her.'

Kirstie took a deep breath, reining Golden Dawn back towards the entrance to the park. Then her face broke into a wide grin. 'No need!' she sighed.

Because Hollywood came dancing and prancing down the hill like she was God's gift. Her silky tail swished; her long mane hung low over her dark eyes. And she swung her rear end as she descended, like a beauty queen sashaying down a catwalk. *Look at me!*

Slowly, slinkily she approached the exhausted riders. Elegantly she turned her head this way and that. *Look at my beautiful arched neck, my high-stepping walk!*

And Kirstie couldn't help her grin from developing into a chuckle. The movie-star horse really did think the world began and ended with her beautiful self.

But, *Get a move on!* Golden Dawn reached out and nipped at Hollywood's round haunch with sharp teeth as the albino glided by. *I have work to do. I can't hang around here no longer!*

Ouch! Hollywood Princess felt the rebuke. She skittered sideways into Taco, who buffeted her back and hurried her up the ramp.

With a rattle and a clang the tailgate was raised and bolted.

Kirstie could see the wounded look on Hollywood's face as she peered out of the back of the trailer. 'Don't look at me!' she laughed. 'I'm not the one who bit your butt!'

That was me! Golden Dawn seemed to say with the toss of her head. She gave the temperamental star the deadeye. *Can't you see, you foolish girl, that the sun's goin' down, and I have a hungry foal to feed back at Half-Moon Ranch!*

3

'You should've seen those horses over at Aspen Park!' Lisa told Hadley as she, Kirstie and he led the three broodmares back to their foals. 'All that spring grass for them to eat and no nuisance dudes coming along to sit on their backs and kick the heck out of 'em!'

The old man smiled as he opened the gate to Pond Meadow. He and Kirstie's down-to-earth friend got along just fine. 'Yeah, I reckon they thought they'd died and gone to hog-heaven!' he agreed.

'Guess who evaded capture until the very last moment,' Kirstie chipped in. Since the last trailer-load of fugitives had got home safely, she felt she could relax and enjoy telling the tale of Hollywood Princess's late appearance.

But she reckoned without Golden Dawn, who was even now straining at the lead-rope in her eagerness to meet up with her hungry foal. 'Hold it, OK!' Kirstie cried, as the mare almost wrenched her arm out of its socket. She struggled to unbuckle the halter, aware that the little sorrel was whinnying for his mom from the far side of the pond.

And as soon as she was free, Golden Dawn took off at a lope around the rim of the pool. She was a fine sight, with her mane flying and the four white socks on her sturdy legs showing up bright in the evening shadows.

Kirstie stood and watched little Tatum totter towards oncoming Golden Dawn. A smile formed on her lips. To her mind, there were few sights more heartwarming than a mare making contact with her offspring.

'Cute!' she sighed, as Tatum's stiff steps took him through a narrow rivulet and up a rough, grassy slope. His large head seemed too heavy for his spindly body; his little ears were pricked forward as he used every muscle to make his way to the familiar warmth and comfort of his mother's presence.

'Made it!' Kirstie sighed as the two finally met up. Golden Dawn and Tatum were maybe fifty yards away, separated from her by a stretch of still, dark green water. The meadow was already in shadow and the air grew quickly cool, but even so she felt a warm glow spread through her body.

Goldie bent her graceful neck to nuzzle at Tatum's face, then she made a series of small nudges with her nose along the foal's neck and back. The mother's stance seemed to show a mixture of concern and impatience: *How did you get along without me? How come you're all covered in dust?*

'Typical mom!' Kirstie murmured, drawing Lisa and Hadley's attention.

'Huh?' Lisa wanted to know what she'd just said.

'Nothing . . . really!' Kirstie blushed, knowing that she would get a hard time from her friend if she owned up to the lump she felt in her throat when she watched Golden Dawn and Tatum together.

'Are you comin' to help Hadley fetch alfalfa for the manger?' Lisa asked, now that both Yukon and Taco had also been reunited with their foals.

'No, I'll stay here a while,' Kirstie decided. A thought floated through her head; had Hadley done what her mom had asked earlier and called the people at the dam to check water levels in Five Mile Creek? But it was too late to ask him as he and Lisa had already headed back to the barn to stack the battered but still functioning pick up with feed.

Sure he did, she told herself, gazing at Tatum's dive for the teat. He splayed his legs, aimed his lips and was soon sucking contentedly. Hadley's the most reliable guy around. He checked that Pond Meadow was safe for the mares and foals; no question.

So the thought had slid from her mind by the time the hay arrived on the back of the truck. She helped Lisa lift it down and together the girls tossed flaps into the metal cage that formed a strong manger by the side of the pond. Soon the mares had come ambling across the meadow and were tugging feed through the gaps.

Munch-munch-munch. Kirstie stood back to enjoy the lazy, grinding sound of the horses' teeth chewing hay. She breathed in the sweet smell, smiled again at the antics of the clumsy foals as they too tried to pull the feed from the manger.

'You're not so hot at that yet,' she told the tiny sorrel.

Wisps of hay were stuck in his fuzzy forelock and trailing from the sides of his mouth. In fact, there was hay anywhere but in his mouth. But at least he was trying.

'. . . Kirstie?' Lisa's voice broke into her happy contemplation. 'Hadley said, do you want a ride back on the pick-up?'

'Oh, no . . . thanks.' Telling them that she would walk back in a while, she edged closer to the feeding horses.

Now was a good time for her to do a little work with Tatum, she decided. And by 'work' she meant simply handling the foal in a special way which was aimed at getting him used to having people around. The technique was called imprinting and had been taught to her by Matt, who had learned it in college. Old cowhands like

Hadley might mock it, but Kirstie was sure that the method did help in the eventual training of the young horse to accept the bit and saddle.

What it took was a gentle but firm approach, and the belief was that you had to start early. As soon as the foal was born, in fact. Right there in the stall where the mare gave birth, you had to step in and bond with the newborn. Rubbing the head and face was the first step, then when he was relaxed and the mare was also happy with what you were doing, you rubbed and massaged each ear. Nostrils were next, then lips, gums and tongue.

'It's called desensitisation,' Matt had explained, working with Taco's second foal, Gulliver, earlier that spring. Gulliver had been born at three a.m. and, as with the mare's first foal, Moonshine, who had died the year before, the imprinting had been introduced right away. 'We're habituating the foal to being handled so that he bonds with us guys as much as he does with his mom. You keep up this rubbing and massaging over the first couple of days, then you stay with it week in, week out. And you always make sure that he knows who's the boss; no headbutting, no kicking allowed.'

Kirstie had listened and learned fast in the dark stall. Her heart had been full of tenderness and amazement. 'It works!' she'd sighed when the dark bay foal had responded to her gentle strokes by getting shakily to his feet and stumbling through the straw to follow her when she got ready to leave.

They'd repeated the training for Butterscotch, Yukon's latest foal, and by the time Tatum's turn came along, Kirstie was beginning to feel like an expert.

It took patience. You didn't have to mind about getting up in the middle of a frosty night and dedicating hour after hour to handling the foals in the draughty barn. Your fingers might be stiff from cold, your eyes might feel like a couple of boiled eggs bulging out of their sockets, but you hung on in there and did what you had to do.

And now, in the late spring, it was pay-off time. After all that imprinting, a foal would come up to you as gladly as he did to his mom. He would let you run your hands all down his back and encircle your hands around his girth. He wore a special, permanent halter without even noticing. And Kirstie could pick up and tap each foot, flex

Tatum's neck and turn his head towards his side; in short, do everything with him that would have to be done when at three years old he became a steady and reliable member of the dude ranch string.

'Good boy!' she soothed as she ran her hands down his knobbly legs. 'You're doin' just great, you hear?'

Tatum lowered his head and squirmed it around to nuzzle her arm. Wisps of hay fell from his mane on to Kirstie's sleeve, where he nibbled at them softly.

Kirstie grinned and put an arm around his willowy neck. 'Not a lot of people know this, but you're my favourite little guy around here!' she whispered.

The sorrel foal was the nicest colour, had the prettiest face, the biggest eyes. And he had a gentle, trusting nature, that touched her deeply.

'OK, we're done!' she sighed after they'd enjoyed the hug; him and her both. 'Get back to the important stuff like eating. I'll see you tomorrow!'

Tatum curled back his lips and snorted, running alongside her as she walked away.

'Hey, didn't you hear me? I said, scoot!' She whooshed him away, back towards his mom.

Not even one more itsy-bitsy rub? he pleaded with his nut-brown eyes.

Kirstie stood hands on hips, a smile playing over her mouth. 'Go!' she insisted.

A snicker from Golden Dawn made him turn and wobble into a dip. He went down on to his knees, shook his head, picked himself up. Then he forgot Kirstie and went scrambling through the thick grass, pushing his way in between Butterscotch and Gulliver at the manger, shoving his rivals out of the way.

'See you tomorrow,' Kirstie repeated with a sigh. A happy sigh, not a sad one. Sometimes her heart was just so full.

'We found this last bunch down by Marshy Meadows!' Charlie told Kirstie and Lisa, who were sitting on the corral fence counting in the cows and calves.

It was a full week later; seven days in which the two dozen new guests to Half-Moon Ranch had become old guests and new friends. Among the visitors for Cattle Week were a doctor, a foodstore manager, a college lecturer and many more who didn't know one end of a cow from the other.

But after this week of chasing calves down culverts and examining hoofprints in the mud beside mountain streams, each and every one was an expert. After all, between them they'd rounded up eighty-five cows and calves and brought them in for tagging.

'. . . Eighty-three, eighty-four, eighty-five!' Lisa yelled out as the gate slammed shut after the last broad black-and-white back had shunted through.

'Yep, eighty-five!' Kirstie confirmed the number of cows. 'But I only got eighty-four calves.'

'Huh!' Matt frowned and climbed up on the fence beside the girls. 'The preg check last fall confirmed that every single cow in the herd was carrying a calf. So what happened to number eighty-five, I wonder?'

Searching closely through the barging, bellowing creatures penned into the corral, Kirstie at last made out an unusually coloured reddish-brown cow who stood in the nearest corner minus her offspring. She'd come in with the last bunch and was one of only two Herefords in the whole herd, so easy to identify. 'Number thirty-one!' She pointed her out and read the yellow tag that had been punched through the brown cow's right ear.

Pulling out a rolled-up sheet from his jeans pocket, Matt scanned the list. 'Like I said, we definitely have this cow down as pregnant early last November. So what happened?'

'Problem?' Sandy asked, striding across the yard towards the noisy corral. She listened carefully to her son's answer, then thought a while. 'Maybe the calf miscarried?' she suggested.

'Or maybe it was born perfectly fine and got left behind during the round-up,' was Kirstie's idea. She pictured a lone calf out on the mountains, calling pitifully for its mom.

Matt shrugged and sighed. 'Possible, I guess.'

No one spoke for a few seconds, then Lisa turned sideways on the fence towards Kirstie. 'How about you and I go take a look?'

'In Marshy Meadows?' Kirstie knew the spot where Charlie and his gang of dudes had found the cows. It was a couple of miles upstream, towards Dorfmann Lake; a wide, gently sloping valley with ponderosa pines running along each ridge. The grass there was rich, there was shelter and plenty of water; ideal territory for cows to graze. 'Hey, yeah, there's a stand of willows in the bottom where a calf could easily get lost and left behind!'

Lisa jumped down from the fence. 'C'mon, what're we waiting for?'

'For Mom to say yes,' Kirstie countered, turning with an inquiring look to face Sandy.

'Yeah, why not?' Agreeing that it was worth a shot, Sandy arranged for Lucky and Hollywood to be saddled up, ready to go. 'I don't like the idea of a calf out there alone come nightfall,' she confessed, waving Lisa and Kirstie off with a warning not to stay out late or take any unnecessary risks. 'The creek in Marshy Meadows feeds directly into Shady River,' she reminded them. 'The meltwater is running down from the peaks pretty fast at this time of year, so don't try crossing the river under any circumstances, OK?'

With a promise to take care, Kirstie and Lisa hit the trail. With fresh horses they knew they could reach the meadow in thirty minutes, scout around and be back in time for supper.

'We're gonna find this baby and when we bring

her back we'll be heroes!' Lisa said, her face alive with anticipation, her green eyes sparkling.

But half an hour later, in the open space of Marshy Meadows, her confidence quickly began to fade.

Kirstie slowed Lucky to a trot and approached the willows by the creek. The bushes were thick and tangled, their leaves shimmering in a gentle breeze. 'I can't see a yard in front of me down here!' she yelled back at Lisa.

'Hey, I saw something move!' Lisa called, trotting Hollywood along the near edge of the willows. She peered into the thicket. 'No, forget it. It's only a deer!'

Disturbed by their voices, the buck crashed out of the bushes head down, his antlers snapping branches as he charged. Then he was clear and leaping out of the valley up on to the western ridge, where he disappeared amongst the pines.

'Let's follow the creek!' Kirstie called. She was having to bend low and shield her head from the slim branches which whipped against her face as Lucky struggled through the willows. 'Look out for fresh hoofprints, OK?'

'Sure!' Lisa's voice was more distant, meaning

that she'd steered Hollywood wide of the thicket. 'Say, what's on that pile of brushwood jammed between those two tall rocks up there?'

Kirstie emerged from the bushes, her face and hands scratched. When she was able to sit upright in the saddle, she saw Lisa pointing to a dam formed out of dead wood at the head of a culvert. There was a thin trickle of water spilling down the rocks from a ledge about twenty feet above the ground, but the area was so shadowy and hidden that it took a while for her to work out what her friend was showing her.

'All I know is that this is called Deadwood Cemetery,' she explained, her eyes scrunched for a better view. 'It took a long time for the timber to pile up that way; the floodwaters dump it when Shady River rises above a certain level.'

'Yeah, yeah, but what's shifting around on top?' Lisa grew more agitated. Hollywood too began to prance nervously and edge away from the culvert.

And now that her eyes had grown used to the gloom, Kirstie could make out the movement Lisa meant. There were definitely creatures up there, standing on top of the high pile of deadwood.

Grey creatures too intent on their own business to remark the presence of intruders.

'Coyotes!' Kirstie whispered. The sound of her own voice made her shiver.

'Oh, gee!' came Lisa's faint response. 'What're they doing?'

'I don't know, but it looks kinda ugly!' Taking a deep breath, Kirstie edged Lucky a little closer. 'I can count four of them!'

'Hold it. Don't get too close!'

She ignored Lisa and pushed on. 'One, two, three, four. They're eating something up there; tearing it apart!'

'Don't tell me!'

The animals standing astride Deadwood Cemetery ripped at a carcass with fierce fangs. They tore and sucked, tossed scraps in the air, plunged back into the bloody mess with ravenous appetites.

Sickened, shuddering with disgust, Kirstie retreated out of the gulley. 'It's the calf,' she confirmed in a flat whisper, her grey eyes wide, her mouth dry.

'Sure?' Lisa stared back.

She nodded.

'So, that accounts for number eighty-five!' Sounding heartless, but in reality as shocked as her friend, Lisa reined her horse back towards the open meadow.

Kirstie followed more slowly. 'Yeah, but why?'

'Why what?'

'Why are the coyotes eating the calf? Did they attack it before or after Charlie and the rest rounded up the bunch that were in here?' Already Kirstie's mind was sharpening up again after the sickening sight.

'What's it matter?' Lisa didn't get it. 'The coyotes are eating the calf; period!'

Still Kirstie puzzled it through. 'Yeah but there's a mystery here. What got into the coyotes that they attacked an animal as big as a calf? Those things are scavengers, they prey on dead meat.'

'You mean, it's not normal for them to attack something that's still breathing!'

'Right!' Kirstie breathed out hard. Then she shuddered again. 'Y'know, they looked like pure evil up there against the sky. I could see the glint in their eyes!'

'You think they went crazy and brought down

the live calf in some kind of frenzy?' The idea made Lisa kick her heels against Hollywood's sides and urge the horse into a lope.

'Crazy coyotes!' Kirstie murmured. 'The sooner we get out of here the better!'

Lucky and Hollywood tried to pick up speed along the valley bottom, but the soft earth sucked at their hooves and dragged them down. They galloped clumsily, ears set back, listening out for the howl of the hungry coyotes from creepy Deadwood Cemetery.

4

'I tell you, I felt sick to my stomach!' Lisa told Matt and Sandy Scott. Her fork hovered over her supper plate, her appetite killed by the afternoon's experience in Marshy Meadows.

'Well, at least you guys accounted for the missing calf,' Matt replied. 'And really, losing one out of eighty-plus ain't the end of the world.'

'It was for the calf in question,' Kirstie put in quietly and seriously. 'Like, literally!'

'The point is, what got into the coyotes?' Pushing her plate away, Lisa appealed to Sandy.

'It's not as if they're short of food at this time of year. So why did they attack and kill the calf, rather than feed off easy stuff like rabbit carcasses?'

'Yeah, it's a bit weird,' Sandy agreed. But she was obviously preoccupied. Like Matt, she was satisfied with the investigations that Kirstie and Lisa had made, even if she wasn't too happy with the outcome.

Lacking much response, Lisa turned to Charlie and Ben, who also sat with the family to eat. 'OK, get this!' she persisted, leaning forward and fixing them with wide eyes. 'If coyotes can turn a little crazy and bring down a four month old calf, what's to stop them from doing the same thing to one of the foals out there in Pond Meadow?'

'Hey, hold on!' The head wrangler rested back on two legs of his chair, wiping his mouth with his napkin. 'That's a big jump you just made. One thing doesn't necessarily follow on from the other.'

'Lisa's not saying it absolutely does.' Kirstie joined in the discussion with more force. 'She's just saying maybe. And I happen to agree with her. I think we should keep an eye on the foals.'

'Yeah well, Charlie can take a walk out there after supper.' Ben stood up and thanked Sandy for the meal. 'Did you hear any more from Waddie Newton?' he asked her in passing.

She nodded. 'It sounds like he's dead set on selling off Aspen Park. I spoke to him earlier today, told him we'd like to keep on renting pasture up there for as long as possible. But he told me he's on the brink of signing a deal with the Denver guy. Come next year, there's likely to be new owners and God knows what kind of plans to develop a leisure facility up there.'

Kirstie frowned. No wonder her mom's mind wasn't on the dead calf. 'What about the National Park people? Don't they have something to say about it?'

'I talked with Smiley Gilpin. The Forest Guard already tried to block the sale because of projected damage to the access roads. From what I hear, they got precisely nowhere. If Waddie is set on selling, there's not a thing they can do.'

'Wow, heavy!' Lisa muttered.

It was the kind of big problem that made Kirstie feel helpless, so she turned to more practical tasks. 'C'mon, Lisa, let's help Charlie out by taking a look at the foals for ourselves.'

'Sure.' Lisa stood up willingly. 'Any excuse to get out of washing dishes!'

'Hey, I know my place!' Charlie grinned. 'Leave the dishes to me, why don't you?'

Joking to ease the Aspen Park situation, the group broke up. Kirstie and Lisa went first to the barn, where they dipped into the feed bin to scoop out pocketfuls of grain pellets for the mares and foals. Then they walked out along Five Mile Creek, past Red Fox Meadow where the ramuda grazed quietly after a hard day's work rounding up the final cattle.

'Jeez, it's cold!' Lisa complained, turning up her collar against the evening breeze.

'You should try wearing thermal underwear,' Kirstie suggested with a sideways look at the light cotton jacket that her friend was wearing. Whenever she came to stay, Lisa never looked equipped for ranch life. She stuck with her fashion items and make-up, even when the temperatures zoomed down each night to way below freezing, as it did at ten thousand feet, even in spring.

'Yeah, and you sound like my grandad!' Lisa

retorted, running ahead over the footbridge which crossed the creek into Pond Meadow. 'It's OK; you can breathe again. I'm counting three foals and three mares, all present and correct!'

The horses in the secluded meadow all raised their heads at the girls' approach.

'Ah, sweet!' Lisa cooed. 'They're comin' over. They must be pleased to see us!'

Taco led the way from the far side of the pond. With little Gulliver in tow she plodded purposefully towards the visitors.

Kirstie grinned at the sight of the dark foal skipping along to keep up with his mom. ' "Pleased to see us" nothin'! They smell grain!'

'Cynic!' Either way, Lisa didn't care, as long as she got a chance to pet and fondle the foals.

A fish jumped at a fly on the surface of the pond, cleared the water, then plopped back in, spreading wide ripples. In the distance, a coyote howled.

As her friend fed Taco and Gulliver their suppertime treats, Kirstie walked to meet Yukon and Butterscotch. The pale fawn paint foal was especially sweet, with unusual blue-grey eyes and a pink muzzle which gave her an albino look.

Mother and offspring quickly gobbled up their share of the pellets and demanded more, so Kirstie laughingly sent them on their way and walked on by the water's edge to seek out Golden Dawn and Tatum.

She spotted the sorrel mare lingering in the shadow of a clump of willows. It was unlike Goldie to hang back. Normally she'd be up at the front, shoving others out of the way. 'What's the problem?' she inquired gently. 'Are you sulking 'cos Yukon and Taco beat you to it?'

The mare hung her head but didn't move. Behind her, the white flash on Tatum's forehead told Kirstie that the foal was also standing deep in the shadows.

'Huh!' Slightly worried, Kirstie moved in closer. Golden Dawn sure looked sorry for herself. And as she drew near, Kirstie saw why.

'Lisa!' She gasped, turned and called to her friend, who came running. By the time Lisa arrived, Kirstie was bending down to inspect the mare's belly. 'Look at this!'

She pointed to a cut just behind the front leg, roughly in the spot where a cinch would tighten. At first Kirstie had supposed that the two-inch gash might have been caused by riding the mare too hard on the trip out to Aspen Park to round up the escaped horses. But that injury would have been a week old by now and this one was much fresher. Blood had only just congealed around it, and the flap of torn skin could still be pressed gently back into place.

'What happened?' Lisa asked with a worried frown. She winced as Kirstie examined the cut and the horse flinched.

'Looks like Goldie got into a fight.'

'With one of the other mares?' Lisa stooped for a closer look.

'I doubt it.' Kirstie shook her head, then stood up straight to cast a glance around the meadow. 'The cut looks as if it was made by something sharp, not a blunt hoof. And if she'd been scrapping with Taco or Yukon, the injury would most likely be on her back.'

'So maybe it was razor wire?' Lisa suggested.

'We don't use it in these meadows,' Kirstie answered, her gaze raking the hillsides, though she didn't really know what she was expecting to see. 'No, my guess is that it's some other kind of animal.'

It was Lisa who put the fear into words. 'You think a coyote snuck in here?'

'Possibly more than one.' Probable even, given what they knew about the crazy bunch at Marshy Meadows. Urged on by their success with the lone calf, the pack could've moved in on the ranch and spotted what looked like equally helpless foals.

'And good old Golden Dawn reared up on her hind legs and fought them off!' Lisa whispered. The shiver that had run through her earlier because of the chill wind came back with a vengeance. 'Oh my!'

'Any mare would give her own life to protect her foal,' Kirstie said. 'If we're right about this, Goldie got off pretty lightly!'

Maybe the coyote they'd heard calling from one of those hills had sneaked into Pond Meadow. Maybe there were four of them or more. She imagined them circling the meadow in the dusk light, waiting for one of the foals to split off from their mom, moving in under cover of the trees.

Perhaps little Tatum had wandered just a yard too far; maybe past this bunch of willows for fresh grass on the slope.

And the nearest coyote had seized his chance. Pounce; a leap from the bushes; two or three smooth, silent bounds towards the helpless foal.

But Goldie would have been even quicker off the mark. She would have sensed the predator with a power even beyond smell or hearing; an instinct which would warn in a split second that her baby was in danger. And she would have been there as the coyote had jumped snarling from his cover. Kirstie pictured her rearing up and striking at him with both front feet while Tatum slid away out of the hunter's reach. Her hooves would have smashed down on top of the coyote. It would have been then that his jaws had snapped and closed on her belly, making this raw tear in her skin.

Kirstie knew the mare would have forgotten the pain in her anger and reared a second time. Her fury to protect her foal would have known no bounds.

And the coyote, realising he'd missed his chance, would've slunk off to join his pack, long tail between his legs, body bruised by the beating he'd taken from the angry mare.

It was a scenario that struck a chill into Kirstie and Lisa's hearts as they stood a while in the darkening meadow, wondering what to do.

Then, recovering their common sense, they ran back to the ranch to bring out Matt and Sandy to check on Golden Dawn's injury.

'It's nothing serious,' Matt insisted. 'The cut doesn't need a suture, and Golden Dawn's up to date with her tetanus jabs. In fact, I'd rather not do anything with it except clean it and keep an eye on the healing process.'

'That's good to hear.' Sandy agreed that they should take no further action. 'And let's hope that the coyote who decided to mess with Goldie learned his lesson good and proper!'

Listening carefully, an idea formed in Kirstie's head. 'Maybe we could check that out,' she said thoughtfully, bringing the details together as she spoke. 'How about me and Lisa camping out tonight to keep guard?'

'In case the coyotes come back for a second attempt?' Sandy's brow wrinkled at the practical steps they would have to take and at the possible risk to the girls. 'You sure you can stand your ground?'

'Sure!' Kirstie tried to sound more confident

than she felt. 'Whoever heard of coyotes attacking people?'

'Hmm.' Sandy looked to Matt for guidance.

'I'd place bets that they won't be back after they failed first time,' said Matt reassuringly.

'Which makes it *not* dangerous for us to camp out and make sure,' Kirstie insisted logically. 'Consider it as us girls having a sleepover out in the open. We'll bring Hershey bars and potato chips . . .'

'. . . Hot chocolate and marshmallows,' Lisa added.

'A tent, sleeping-bags, flashlights.' Kirstie built up the list of things they might need.

Matt shrugged then smiled. 'Hey, I just thought of something. You remember the field-study I did with college over New Year? We were up in Alaska studying the habits of grizzlies, and I came back with a couple of pairs of infra-red goggles we'd used to watch the bears' after-dark activities. I guess I may still have them in my closet.'

'So we could use them to spot coyotes!' Lisa sounded enthusiastic about being able to see in the dark. 'Cool!'

'Mom?' Kirstie waited for the all-important agreement.

'Yeah, why not?' Knowing that, as Kirstie said, coyotes never attacked humans, Sandy couldn't see any real harm in it, as long as Lisa and Kirstie followed the usual advice to stay out of trouble. 'Rather you than me in these below-zero temperatures,' she shivered, leading the group out of Pond Meadow and leaving the mares and colts to settle back into a last little serious grazing before night fell.

'I told you: thermal underwear!' Kirstie herself was finding it hard to stop her teeth from chattering. And she was wearing three layers of clothing plus a padded jacket.

'T-t-too late!' Lisa sighed, her teeth knocking together, her jaw rigid with cold.

It was two a.m. They'd been camping out for four hours and not seen or heard a single suspicious thing.

'Try wrapping your sleeping-bag around your shoulders,' Kirstie suggested in the pitch-dark.

'I am already!'

Kirstie shone her flashlight on Lisa who was

huddled in the corner of the tent. 'Oh yeah, sorry.'

For a few seconds there was silence, except for the sound of the wind in the ponderosa pines and the occasional hoot of an owl. Then: 'Do we have any hot chocolate left in the Thermos?'

'Nope. You asked me that three times already.' Fumbling on the groundsheet for the infra-red goggles which Matt had given them, Kirstie unzipped the tent flap for a quick reconnaissance of the meadow.

It was weird being able to see clearly in the middle of the night. There was the pond, still and glassy in the moonlight; there were the pine trees rustling in the wind.

And the horses lay undisturbed in the shelter of the willows, their foals by their sides, twitching and sighing in their sleep.

'Try to get some rest,' Kirstie suggested to Lisa. 'I can keep watch for a couple of hours, then we could switch around.'

'No chance.' Lisa crept alongside her, fixing her goggles around her head. 'Y' know, maybe we were wrong about the coyotes. It don't look to me like there's any wildlife action out there.'

True, it was eerily quiet. But coyotes were stealthy creatures. They would win prizes for creeping about unnoticed. Any time now, one could leap out of the straggly willows.

'Maybe we even made a mistake about them attacking the calf.' A new possibility entered Lisa's head for the first time. 'Is there any way that calf could've been dead before the coyotes happened to come across it?'

'Like, it climbed the rock by Deadwood Cemetery, stumbled, maybe broke its leg?' Kirstie took this up. 'So it was stranded up there and starved to death?'

'Or else it was stillborn.'

'No, it was too big to be newborn. But y'know, you're right. If the calf died of natural causes, like breaking a leg or drowning in Shady River, those coyotes were only doin' what they normally do, which is to feed off dead carcasses!'

'Why didn't we think of that sooner?'

Kirstie turned into the tent to look at Lisa, who stared back at her through the unattractive, round-rimmed goggles. Suddenly, she felt a small curl of laughter begin to work its way up into her throat.

'What's so funny?' Lisa objected.

The urge to laugh grew stronger. 'Nothing. Those goggles . . . I mean, don't mind me . . . hah! . . . Oh my God!' Rolling over to hold her stomach, Kirstie gave way to hysterics.

'You can't talk!' Lisa protested, trying to pull Kirstie into a sitting position. 'You look pretty stupid yourself . . . ha-ha-hah!'

Soon they were both rolling around the dark tent, unable to keep a hold of themselves.

Then outside, a horse whinnied, shrill and loud.

'Sshh!' Kirstie sat up straight. She froze and listened.

Lisa poked her head out of the tent. 'It's Golden Dawn!'

'What d'you see? Coyotes?'

'Zilch. Not a thing.'

'But there must be something out there.' Kirstie forced herself out of the opening and stood up outside the tent. She could see the sorrel mare standing to attention over a still sleepy Tatum, her ears pricked towards the forested hillside, her head raised high to sniff the night air. 'I'm gonna take a look!'

'No, Kirstie! . . . OK then; wait for me!' Scrambling out after her, Lisa followed. They trod cautiously around the pond until they came to the place where Golden Dawn stood.

'What is it, girl?' Kirstie raised a hand to stroke the horse's neck. 'There, take it easy. Leave this to us.'

'Kirstie, hold it. Don't you think . . . ? Oh, what the heck! When did you ever listen to *me*?'

Kirstie had gone on regardless, able to see clear as day through the goggles, picking out a patch of dense shadow under the trees as the spot which had bothered the mare. And by now, both Yukon and Taco were also awake, roused by Golden Dawn and determinedly standing guard over their two foals.

Lisa stumbled after Kirstie, her protests falling away. 'Hey, there's something up in that tree!' she squeaked suddenly, catching Kirstie's arm and pointing to the left.

Kirstie swung round. Lisa was right; a creature had moved up out of sight, making the lower branches sway. 'Not coyote then,' she muttered. Those guys stuck to the ground to stalk their prey, hiding among bushes and in the long grass.

'It's big!' Lisa warned in the same strangled voice.

'Did you see it?'

'No, but look at the weight of it. See those branches bend! Oh God, what is it?'

Slowly Kirstie tiptoed towards the tree. 'I think it's up in that fork in the main trunk, whatever it is!'

'Oh Jeez . . . oh, don't go any closer!' Lisa implored. 'Let's just round up the horses and take them down to Red Fox Meadow. They'll be safe there!'

'We can't do that. No halters, no lead-ropes,' Kirstie murmured. The more Lisa lost her head, the more determined she was to keep hers. 'Listen; I think it's a bear!'

'Bear?' Lisa's croak fell away to a groan.

'Yeah. If it is, you know what to do?' Kirstie didn't take her eyes off the tree for a second. By now she could make out a solid blob squatting in the darkest part of the tree. 'Never run from a bear, OK? You need to stand still.'

'Yeah, yeah, I know. You stretch your arms out wide and make like you're really giant-size. Officially the bear grows scared of you and runs away.' Lisa sounded like she didn't believe a word.

'If it's a bear, I'm not worried.' Not in theory anyway. Generally, bears didn't attack humans or horses. In fact, they were peaceable vegetarians, unless you happened to come between them and their cubs.

'Me neither!' Lisa squeaked.

'Yes, there it is!' Kirstie had walked full circle around the tree and stared up at the fork in the trunk. She was pointing at a fully grown, honey-coloured bear with a big, square head and front paws the size of frying-pans.

The bear gazed down at them. He squatted heavily on his haunches, his small eyes sparkling like chips of coal in his pale face, his coat thick and matted, his claws glinting.

'See!' Kirstie whispered. 'There's no need to be scared. He won't harm us!'

Hhh-rrr-uughhh-aaagh! The bear's roar came from deep in his chest. It began as a hiss and ended like a roll of thunder.

'*Waagh!*' Kirstie jumped and screamed. So much for the tough-it-out, guard-the-horses theory.

'Scoot!' Lisa cried.

And they turned and ran. As the thousand-pound bear began to descend from its tree, snapping branches as thick as a man's arm as it came, the girls broke every rule in the book.

'Wait for me!' Kirstie yelled as Lisa covered the ground faster than a greyhound. Her horse protector partner had already reached the fence and vaulted clean over it.

'Get a gun! Shoot it!' Lisa cried, making hell-for-leather for the ranch along the creek trail.

'It's OK, he's not following us!' Kirstie risked a glance over her shoulder. In the weird infra-red rays produced by the goggles, she could see the bear lumbering in the opposite direction up the hill. Despite his clumsy build, he too was moving at high speed.

'Help! Somebody, come quick!' In no mood for reassurance, Lisa followed her instinct to get the heck out of there. Never mind that she stumbled over the undone laces of her trainers, or that by the time they reached the ranch house, Kirstie had already slowed to a walk; Lisa didn't plan to stop running until she had four solid walls around her and at least two adults, preferably with a gun apiece, to defend her from the big, bad bear in the woods.

5

'Coyotes don't do that,' Hadley asserted, sinking his teeth into a chunky bacon sandwich.

He was eating breakfast in the grey dawn light of Sunday morning, listening to Lisa and Kirstie's account of their night-time adventure.

'Don't do what?' Lisa challenged. She'd just finished imitating the thunderous roar of the bear in the tree and exaggerating his size by around fifty per cent for dramatic effect. Then she'd gone on to question the earlier coyote theory.

'They don't attack full-grown mares. Leastways,

I ain't never seen such a thing.' The old man chomped on as he talked. 'Come to that, I didn't reckon they'd brought down that calf in Marshy Meadows neither.'

Kirstie tutted. 'Why didn't you say so?'

He eyed her narrowly over the rim of his coffee mug, which he'd raised steadily to his mouth. 'I don't recollect you askin' my opinion.'

'So I'm asking now.' Kirstie wasn't put off by Hadley's wry put-down. 'In your opinion, what happened to the calf?'

'Could be any one of a number of things,' he shrugged. 'Could've been rejected by its mom and starved to death. Could've broke a leg and got left behind.'

'That's exactly what I said!' Lisa broke in. 'I reckon the coyotes couldn't believe their luck when they came across the carcass!'

'Hmm.' Kirstie didn't enjoy being proved wrong. 'So what injured Golden Dawn if it wasn't a coyote?'

Lisa spread her hands, palms upwards, as if the answer was obvious. 'The bear, of course!'

'Nope.' Hadley finished off his sandwich and swallowed the last of his coffee. 'No way would the bear move in on a mare. Especially not a tough customer like the sorrel. The truth is, he was most likely more scared of her than the other way around. And he gets plenty to eat, scavenging around our grain bins, so no way was he hungry enough to be any threat to the foals.'

Kirstie had to admit to herself the truth of all this. Ashamed now of her panic the previous night, she waited in silence to hear the remainder of the old wrangler's well-informed point of view.

'Yeah, what went off out there in Pond Meadow was most likely some small domestic between the three mares. Golden Dawn and Tatum only just joined the rest, didn't they? Yukon and Taco wouldn't take kindly to the newcomer trying to shove her way up the peckin' order. So a well-aimed nip with the teeth wouldn't go amiss. Then maybe the dispute got out of hand and one of the two mares inflicted a mite more damage than she'd intended. Result: a little torn flesh and a wounded ego for Golden Dawn. No more, no less.'

'Huh.' Matt's grunt from across the breakfast table showed that he agreed with Hadley. 'Drama over. End of story.'

Just then the phone rang.

'Get that, someone!' Sandy called from upstairs.

So Kirstie leaned back in her chair to pick up the receiver and take the call. 'Hey, Charlie,' she said, remembering that Saturday had been the young wrangler's night off and that he'd driven into town to visit friends. She thought his voice sounded strange. 'You hung-over or something?'

'No. Listen, Kirstie, this is real important. Are the mares and foals still out in Pond Meadow?'

'Sure.' Yeah; now she was certain that what she was picking up in Charlie's rushed tone was urgency. 'Where are you? What's the problem?'

'I'm at Steve Winwood's place in San Luis. We've just been talking. You know Steve works up at Dorfmann?'

'Nope.' Kirstie had no idea who Steve Winwood was or where he worked. But the name of the lake rang alarm bells. 'Dorfmann?' she repeated it out loud and saw a grain of anxiety appear in Hadley's eyes. Meanwhile, she heard her mom's footsteps coming downstairs.

'Yeah, listen good. You gotta take those horses

out of Pond Meadow, like fast! Within the next half hour!'

She glanced at her watch and read seven-thirty. 'Is this something to do with the dam?'

'Yep. Steve's boss chose eight a.m as the time to open the sluice gates and let out the overspill.'

Kirstie stood up jerkily. 'You sure about that?'

'One hundred per cent certain,' Charlie told her. 'Steve's standing here right now if you don't believe me.'

'No, no, I believe you! Thanks, Charlie, I'll tell Mom right away.' Putting down the phone, she pivoted to face the door.

'Overspill!' Hadley said, before Kirstie had time to open her mouth.

She nodded.

Sandy understood right away from the few spoken words and the tension in the room what was going on. 'But Hadley, didn't you check?'

Slowly, with a deep frown, the old man shook his head. 'No, ma'am.'

'But I asked you to call Dorfmann a week ago; was it safe to put the mares and foals into Pond Meadow, or was there gonna be any chance of a flash flood from the dam!' Sandy's normally healthy complexion had turned pale.

'I'm sorry, I don't recall you telling me to do that.' Helplessly Hadley shook his head.

Kirstie could have stepped in then and said, 'Yeah, I remember! It was just after Matt crashed the pick-up and the horses were all heading up to Aspen Park. It was on the to-do list Mom gave you!' But she didn't open her mouth. Instead she glanced again at her watch and saw the second-hand ticking steadily round the dial. 'Mom, we've gotta move the horses!' she insisted.

'Yes, you and Lisa run for headcollars and lead-ropes,' Sandy instructed. 'And don't panic. It may be that the engineers up at Dorfmann only release a little snowmelt into the river. Not enough to affect the levels in the tributaries. With luck, Five Mile Creek won't burst its banks and Pond Meadow won't be affected.'

This was what Kirstie tried to think as she and Lisa ran to the tack-room for the equipment they needed.

Sure; that particular meadow was low-lying, which was one reason they stuck mainly to keeping the horses in Red Fox Meadow, with Pond Meadow only used as a reserve pasture. But there was a lot of waterway between here and Dorfmann Dam five miles upstream. Plenty of time for the snowmelt released from the enormous man-made lake to disperse along Shady River and all the hundreds of small creeks feeding in and out of it.

'How often does Dorfmann cause the meadow here to flood?' Lisa asked, unhitching headcollars from a hook.

'Maybe a couple of times every year,' Kirstie replied, trying to keep her anxiety under wraps. 'I guess Mom just reckons we'd better be safe than sorry.'

'Grandpa reckons we got more snowfall than normal this winter, though.' Lisa considered the possibilities. 'Which means more snowmelt come spring, which presumably is why Charlie just made that phone call!'

'Gee, thanks for making me feel better!' Kirstie hurried out with her share of the headcollars, slinging them into the back of the waiting pick-up. She climbed in and hauled Lisa up after her. Inside the cab, Matt was at the wheel, with Ben and Sandy squeezed into the passenger seat.

'OK?' Matt yelled back at them, roaring the

engine, ready to set off for the low-lying meadow.

Kirstie gave the go-ahead, then clung on as the pick-up jerked into action. She and Lisa squatted in the back, heads down and baseball caps pulled well forward to shield themselves from a cold wind and a few drops of rain that had begun to fall from clouds blowing in from the mountains. The pick-up jolted and rattled along Five Mile Creek trail, past Red Fox Meadow and round a couple of sharp twists in the track until it reached the more secluded pasture where the mares and foals were kept.

'Oh, great!' Raking the meadow for the whereabouts of the horses, Lisa spotted them at the furthest possible distance from the gate. 'It's already a quarter off eight!'

'C'mon, let's go!' Kirstie was the first to leap out of the truck with the headcollars.

'We need a plan,' Sandy broke in. 'Kirstie, you go for Golden Dawn while Lisa tries to get a lead-rope on Tatum. Matt and I will work to bring Yukon and Butterscotch out. Ben, can you handle both Taco and Gulliver?'

Everyone listened, nodded, then set out across the rough meadow.

'Just pray this goes without a hitch!' Kirstie whispered, though already she could see the three mares lifting their heads and sensing something amiss. Horses were amazing, the way they picked up on human stress, growing suddenly alert and wary at the least little problem. And this was a big problem, communicating itself first to Taco, then to Yukon and then to Golden Dawn furthest away from the gate.

'All we need now is this rain!' Lisa looked up at the heavy grey sky, allowing the cold drops to splash on to her cheeks. As often with the weather in the Rockies, sunshine could turn to storm within minutes, and just as quickly clear again.

'If you don't like the weather in Colorado, just wait five minutes!' Kirstie muttered a reminder that things could swiftly change. She was more worried about the horses than about getting wet, so she was pleased to see Taco, the black-and-white mare, trotting willingly enough across the meadow towards them with little Gulliver close behind.

Ben spotted them too and approached quickly and calmly. He crossed the narrow footbridge over the creek, halters and lead-ropes slung over one shoulder, stopping at a distance of ten yards and waiting patiently for the mare and foal to come up to him. He already had the collar in place around Taco's head by the time Sandy and Matt cut around the near side of the pond to catch Yukon and the paint foal, while Lisa and Kirstie split off in the opposite direction in search of Golden Dawn and Tatum.

'Wouldn't you just know it!' Lisa groaned, seeing the sorrel mare toss her head in defiance and begin to stride away towards the far fence.

Kirstie broke into a run, sprinting around the rim of the pond with the wind and rain driving against her back. She felt the cold blast cut through her sweatshirt and padded vest, and was aware that her wet jeans already clung uncomfortably to her legs. 'Here, girl!' she called to Golden Dawn as she ran.

But the stubborn mare had seen the ropes and halters – probable signs of having to do some work – and no way was she being brought in willingly. Her walk along the fence perimeter broke into a steady trot, pausing only to check that Tatum was close on her heels.

'Come back!' Lisa wailed as the distance

between horses and pursuers increased. She recognised the hopelessness of trying to catch up on foot, stopped and sighed helplessly.

So, as the others managed to clip lead-ropes on to Yukon, Butterscotch, Taco and Gulliver, Kirstie and Lisa seemed further than ever from leading Golden Dawn and Tatum to safety. Ben was over the footbridge with Taco and Gulliver, running along between them on to the higher ground of Five Mile Creek trail. Behind him, struggling by the gate to persuade Yukon that leaving the meadow was for her own good, Sandy held tight to the rope and urged the paint horse forward.

Battered by the rain, Kirstie pushed wisps of dripping hair from her cheeks and plodded on after Golden Dawn. She'd felt a small tingle of alarm as she'd watched Ben cross the footbridge with Taco and Gulliver: it seemed to her that the water level in the creek had already risen further up the wooden posts supporting the bridge and was now washing in amongst the base of the willow bushes that lined the banks. And the current in the creek was rapid, washing against grey-pink boulders, slapping with a force that suggested the banks would do well to hold.

'Here, Goldie!' she called out, stuffing one hand into her pocket as though it bulged with a special treat for the dripping mare. In fact, there'd been no time to collect grain from the bin before they'd jumped into the pick-up.

The trick fooled no one; instead, the sorrel mare and her foal kept their distance, trotting around the edge of the meadow, half disappearing into a swirl of driving rain.

When they came back into view, the harsh flurry of raindrops had passed clear over the meadow and was pounding on towards the ranch. The soaked ground sucked at the horses' hooves, slowing them down as they wheeled away from the swirling creek and backtracked the way they had come.

Shadowing them, Lisa almost overbalanced in the mud. Her feet skidded and she clung on to Kirstie. 'Sorry!'

'That's OK. Lisa, we've gotta get these two out of here!' No doubt about it now; the water level in the creek was definitely rising. It was within twelve inches of covering the bridge, looking more dangerous by the second. Yet Kirstie knew that when the effect of opening Dorfmann Dam eventually kicked in, the flash flood it created could well be twenty times worse.

Other animals seemed to recognise it too. Whether they could hear the swell of water rising and roaring down rocky channels a couple of miles upstream, or whether some other instinct told them to flee, small creatures emerged in panic from the banks and from amongst thickets, abandoning their dens to scurry uphill. They included rabbits and black squirrels, tiny shrews and deer mice, even a thickset, clumsy badger who clawed his way out of his burrow, poked his striped black-and-white head into the daylight and stomped up the slope to safety.

Then a deer broke cover from the willows and crashed into the meadow fence in his frenzy. His heavy antlers butted against the planks of wood, stunning him until he had time to get his bearings, run again at the obstacle and this time clear it with ease. Then he was gone, into the ponderosa pines, heading along Meltwater Trail towards Miners' Ridge.

The deer's route crossed Goldie's path and brought her up short. It gave Kirstie time to close in on the mare, who turned her head from the fleeing buck to Kirstie with a wild roll of her eyes. The whites showed; she flared her nostrils and snorted in fear.

'You see!' Kirstie said, her voice low and urgent. 'Trust me, we gotta get out of here!'

As Golden Dawn hesitated, her body quivering from head to foot, Kirstie was able to move in, talking all the while.

'This place isn't safe. You hear the water rushing downstream yet? That's snowmelt from the dam. You and Tatum don't want to get left behind now that the others have gone. They know what's good for them, see?'

She felt a moment of triumph as she edged close enough to loop her arm under the mare's neck and slip the headcollar over her nose. Instantly she fastened the buckle and clipped the lead-rope into place. 'Good girl!' she breathed.

'Good job!' Lisa called, able to move in on Tatum now that the mother was caught. 'How much time do we have?'

'Five minutes. We gotta move fast!' Aware that Lisa had made progress with Tatum, Kirstie eased Golden Dawn across the meadow towards the fast-disappearing footbridge. Mud oozed around her boots; rain ran down the back of her neck and dripped from the end of her nose.

'Wait for us!' Lisa gasped. Somehow in the chase after the horses, her cap had blown off, and now her auburn curls had turned black and were flattened against her skull. Fear made her tug too hard at Tatum's rope, causing the foal to rear up and shy away.

'Just keep moving!' Kirstie's heart was in her mouth as the minutes ebbed away. Beyond the creek, on the higher trail leading up the opposite hillside to the guest cabins, Sandy, Matt and Ben stood with the rescued horses.

'OK, we're with you!' Lisa promised.

So Kirstie struggled on through the rain with Golden Dawn, gritting her teeth at the rising creek water, praying that the threatened, fully-blown flash flood didn't materialise after all.

'Easy, girl!' she whispered to the mare as they tried to set foot on the boards of the footbridge. The current had reached the top of the banks to each side and was spilling out on to the meadow, submerging green grass and bright yellow mallows that grew by the creek. Underwater, the flowers looked like shining gold coins from a spilled pirates' hoard amongst the weeds.

The sorrel horse hated the strange sight of water reflecting her own shadowy image as she stepped on to the bridge. As she stamped her objection, the image splintered into a thousand liquid fragments.

And the current was strong, though it only reached Kirstie's ankles as she carried on leading Golden Dawn. It brought light driftwood down from the aspen stand immediately upstream of Pond Meadow - slim branches of willow,

discarded pine planks, tangles of dead twigs and black brushwood.

Worse, Kirstie picked up an extra sound as she fought to cross the bridge. Above the rush of wind and raindrops, she heard a distant roaring sound that was unmistakeably floodwater.

'They opened the dam!' she cried back at Lisa, fighting Goldie with all her strength.

The mare had responded to the sound of the oncoming flood with sheer terror, raising herself up on her hind legs, pawing the air with her hooves.

'Oh, Jeez! Oh, help!' Lisa's voice was panic-stricken. 'Tatum, keep still! . . . Kirstie, help!'

'I can't!' At last Golden Dawn came down on to all-fours, crashing against the bridge rail and making it split into two. Kirstie had to get her across double-quick.

'Tatum's wriggling out of his halter!'

'Hold on to him if you can. Wait there. I'll be back!'

The roar grew louder, accompanied by the scraping, thudding sound of loose boulders carried along on the furious current. *Boom!* The force of the flood smashed against an immoveable cliff; the water echoed and curled around the rock, kept coming inexorably towards Pond Meadow.

'Mom! Matt!' Kirstie yelled, her voice sounding lost under crazy nature's game. 'Come and get Goldie! I have to go help Lisa!'

Figures came running down the slope as the water continued to rise. With a strong slap on the rump, Kirstie sent the mare stumbling on.

Then she turned to face upstream – and had to cling on to the one remaining wooden rail for support.

'Kirstie, Tatum got away!' Lisa cried from somewhere out of the corner of her vision.

Kirstie stood petrified. Turned to stone was how it felt. She was staring at an eight foot wall of water, sweeping down the route of Five Mile Creek. A tidal wave. A flood so terrifying as it bounced boulders, flattened willows, roared on towards her, that it literally paralysed her and took away all power to act.

The wall of water tore along the bed of the stream, scattering debris to either side, pushing a curling, foaming wave ahead of it. One hundred yards away, unstoppable. It channelled itself between two cliffs, emerged with a rush of triumph, thundered onwards.

'Kirstie!' Lisa screamed. 'Oh God, Kirstie, help!'

6

Before she knew it, Kirstie had sent Golden Dawn off towards her brother.

'Get her out of here!' she yelled, turning to cross back over the flooded bridge.

'Not without you!' Matt insisted, reaching out to grab her by the arm.

The wall of water ate up the ground, travelling at terrifying speed. Once it came within striking distance, nothing moved fast enough to get out of its way or was strong enough to withstand its force. It flung huge logs to one side like matchsticks, swamped the willows, tore them up by the roots and tumbled them down the narrow channel between two rocks, not fifty yards from where Matt and Kirstie stood.

'No, Matt, I can take care of myself. I have to help Lisa and Tatum!' She whipped her arm away just in time, dodging back over the bridge, almost deafened by the roaring flood. The sound, the sight, the smell, was overpowering.

And there was Lisa, sprawled on the ground, opening her mouth to yell something that Kirstie couldn't make out. Tatum's halter and lead-rope snaked across the grass. The foal himself was free but down on his knees, struggling to get back up before the deluge struck.

Kirstie's brain seized up under pressure and she clicked into survival mode. Splashing knee-deep through the building surge of water, she made it back to the meadow and staggered to pull Lisa to her feet.

'I can't swim!' Lisa confessed, terror in her eyes as she clung to Kirstie.

'Jeez!' Kirstie never knew this about her best friend. Here they were, standing sodden in a rainstorm, facing a tidal wave of meltwater, and

Lisa was telling her for the first time that she'd never taken swimming lessons as a kid. 'Now's the time to learn!' she quipped grimly.

The floodwater had emerged from the rock channel and swept on. Hitting the fence at the far end of Pond Meadow, it tore the posts from the ground and swirled out across the pasture, followed by a second, still bigger wave.

'Keep hold of me, OK! Whatever happens, don't let go!' Kirstie instructed Lisa, torn now between trying to make it back across the bridge and following the foal. She could see him stand, turn his head in the direction of his mom, open his mouth and whinny. If they attempted to reach him, would there be time to grab his headcollar, loop it around his neck and drag him away from the creek towards higher ground?

'Let's give it a try!' Lisa read her mind and made a move to pull Kirstie towards Tatum.

The rush of water killed all other sound. It gobbled up the land and spread into every crevice.

Kirstie nodded and scrambled in the direction of the helpless foal.

That was moments before the water hit, when

she could still feel the ground beneath her feet and the breath hadn't been knocked out of her body by the brute force of the wave.

It crashed into her with indescribable power. She felt the water smash against her and topple her, felt the current pull her down and swirl her in its brown depths before it released her and sent her bobbing to the surface like a cork.

'Lisa!' she screamed when she reappeared. The wave had torn her friend away.

A log twenty feet long swept towards her, spiky branches twisting and turning. She had to duck down and dive under it, escaping its clutch by inches. When she resurfaced and gulped in air, she still had to fight the current with all her might.

'Lisa!' Tossing her hair from her face, she looked desperately in every direction.

The swirling surface remained unbroken. How long had Lisa been underwater? Where was the current taking her?

'Over there!' Matt had hold of Golden Dawn on Five Mile Creek trail. There was something dreamlike and unreal about seeing them there on dry land while she herself struggled to keep her head above water. He was pointing downstream, past the by-now invisible bridge, towards the tips of some willow bushes which the flood hadn't uprooted and washed away.

And Kirstie could see a dark head break the surface and an arm come out of the water in an effort to catch hold of a branch. She judged that Lisa was about thirty yards away and that she would have to swim diagonally across the current to reach her. Difficult, but possible, she reckoned, so she struck out, partly using the current, partly fighting to cut across it.

Her arms and legs ached, her lungs were bursting. The ice-cold, muddy water filled her mouth and felt as if it was pulling her whole body apart. But she fought it, made headway and finally swam to join Lisa.

'Hang on!' she instructed.

Head back, arms flailing, Lisa made contact with a sturdier branch belonging to a sole aspen tree. With Kirstie's help, she managed to wedge herself against it, chest high out of the rushing water.

'OK?' Kirstie too hung on to the tree to stabilise herself.

Coughing, Lisa nodded. Her eyes had taken on a glazed look; shock setting in after the terror of almost drowning. And the icy water would be making her temperature zoom down, Kirstie knew. Soon she would be hypothermic and slipping into unconsciousness.

'Stay awake!' she yelled, swinging round against the current to face Lisa and make eye contact. 'You hear me? You don't go to sleep, even if that's what you feel like doing!'

Wearily, head swaying forward, Lisa promised to try. 'What about Tatum?' she gasped.

'Never mind!' Later would be time for them to think about the foal. They still had to get Lisa out of this fix.

'Kirstie!' As the swell of water died down, Matt's voice reached them. 'Can you hang on?'

'For how long?' Still the current tugged at them and huge pieces of driftwood sailed perilously close. Lisa's head was sagging forward and Kirstie had to pin her against the fork of the aspen to stop her from slipping away.

'Not long!' Matt's struggle to hold on to Golden Dawn continued. Behind him, Ben and Sandy had tethered the other horses and were running to join him. 'Until the flood passes by; maybe another minute!'

Kirstie turned to Lisa. 'You hear that? We'll be out of here in under sixty seconds. You have to hang on, OK?'

Lisa raised her head, her eyes unfocussed. 'I don't know if I can make it.'

'Sure you can! The water level's falling, see? A few more seconds, that's all.'

Up on the hill, Matt's fight with Goldie had ended in victory for the horse. She'd jerked her head so hard that the lead-rope had burned his palms and finally forced him to let go. And now Golden Dawn came slithering through the mud, hurtling down to the water's edge, crying out shrilly for her lost foal.

It made Kirstie yell out for them not to let the mare swim out into the floodwater. Who knew what the currents were like, or what loose boulders or branches might crash into her if she took the plunge.

Sandy and Matt scrambled down the slope and came alongside the horse, grabbing on to her headcollar and lead-rope, digging in their heels and pulling with all their might.

'Tatum!' The struggle on the bank penetrated Lisa's dulled brain and made her realise that the foal must be missing. Why else would Golden Dawn be risking her life by trying to swim across the flood? 'Oh, Kirstie, what did I do? I let Tatum get away. It's all my fault!'

'Hold it!' Kirstie fought to keep her friend wedged against the tree, willing the overspill from the dam to stop. Her body was turning numb, her actions growing slow and clumsy, but second by second she could've sworn that the current was lessening, the level falling.

And then, almost as suddenly as it had appeared, the flood ceased. Water stopped crashing through the narrow rocky channel upstream and receded from the meadow, draining back in muddy swirls into the creek. It left the trunks of half-decayed trees stranded on the flattened grass, and giant branches jammed against rocks.

'Thank God!' Kirstie breathed as the water level dropped below her waist. Soon she could unhitch Lisa's arms from the fork in the aspen tree and take her weight. Her sodden clothes felt suddenly heavy; her legs trembled as she made contact with the ground and staggered to drag Lisa towards the bridge.

On the far bank, meanwhile, Sandy and Ben had got control of Golden Dawn by anchoring her lead-rope around the trunk of a tree. The poor horse fought and kicked, but no way was she going to be able to break loose again.

Straightaway, Sandy strode down the slope to help Kirstie with Lisa. She waded into the water, arms held wide for balance, careful to avoid the drifting debris. 'Here, give me your hand!' she told the half-conscious girl, and she draped Lisa's arm around her shoulder so that between them Kirstie and she could support her full weight.

'It's OK, we're gonna make it!' Breathless, exhausted, traumatised, Kirstie stumbled through the receding flood. Everything had happened so fast, there had been so much sudden danger that only now was she beginning to realise how lucky they'd been to survive.

'Yes, and we only lost one foal.' Sandy too was grateful as they walked Lisa to safety. The horses up on the trail were quietening down as nature loosed them all from its grip. The worst of the flood had passed, even the lashing rain was starting to ease.

Poor Tatum. Without expressing how she felt, Kirstie took a glance over her shoulder at the grim battlefield scene behind. Fence posts lay broken and scattered over the meadow, whole trees were upturned, their roots torn from the ground. And the floodwater still rested in dark pools in the hollows and dips in the ground. The pond too had broken its bank and lost its neat round shape, spreading into low-lying areas and washing up against the surviving fence at the far side of the field.

There was no foal out there. No skinny survivor with stick-like legs taking refuge beside a rock, his sorrel coat soaked, the flash on his forehead signalling that he had made it through the disaster.

'We only lost Tatum!' Faintly Lisa echoed Sandy's words.

Kirstie looked at her friend's wet face and saw tears.

She held back the welling sensation in her own eyes and stumbled on. *Poor Tatum. Poor Lisa.* Though it was no one's fault exactly, it felt like it would be a long time before those involved would ever be able to forgive themselves.

'Let's face it, things could've turned out a whole lot worse,' Matt insisted.

How? was Kirstie's silent question. Even though they were all safely back at the house, had showered and dressed in warm, dry clothes, her shocked mind couldn't erase the sight of the wall of water crashing down on her, or that last glimpse of Tatum struggling to rise from his knees.

It was two hours since the disaster had occurred. Charlie had called to confirm that the overspill from Dorfmann Dam was complete. Sandy had contacted Lisa's mom, Bonnie, who was this minute driving out from San Luis to Half-Moon Ranch. The rescued horses were safely stalled in the barn.

'I mean, we have to get over what happened to Tatum and count our blessings.' Determined to put the incident behind them, Matt did his best to jolt Lisa and Kirstie out of their distress. 'We saved five out of six horses and no one got injured, did they? Besides, Lisa got a crash course in staying afloat!'

'Not funny, Matt,' Kirstie muttered. But she felt guilty for pulling the mood back down. Sure, they should be grateful. It was like he said; human lives could've been lost. They could so easily have been sitting here now minus Lisa, waiting to break the tragic news to Bonnie Goodman.

But they weren't. Lisa sat opposite Kirstie at the kitchen table, her round face pale and strained, but seemingly none the worse for her icy dip.

'Where did you last see Tatum?' Lisa whispered to Kirstie, as the adults went off on their own tack.

'Not far from where he broke free. When the flood came crashing down, I didn't have the time to look and find out what happened to him. I was too busy trying to keep hold of you!'

'So you think he got swept away?'

Kirstie nodded. 'I guess.'

'But you didn't actually see it?' Lisa pressed urgently to discover a certainty amongst all the fears and doubts.

'Like I said, I was fighting for our lives, period.'

'So there's a chance he survived?'

'Not really. Not when you stop and think about

it.' A deluge of fast-flowing water, a weak little body buffeted and swept away by its force. A few moments of struggle before the flood closed over his head. 'He wouldn't have suffered for long,' she murmured sadly. 'But I guess we'll never know for sure.'

'And that's it? End of story?' Lisa couldn't let it drop. Tears came back into her eyes, but this time they were tears of helpless frustration.

Not quite. The meltwater that had claimed the foal wouldn't want to keep him forever. It would carry the broken body downstream and then eventually ditch it on some lonely bank; maybe before Five Mile Creek joined Brown Bear River, maybe long after. Sooner or later, the corpse would snag on a branch or be washed up in the mud. Coyotes prowling on a nearby ridge would smell its presence and silently, stealthily descend . . .

'I need some fresh air!' Kirstie said quickly, standing up and heading for the porch. Here she paused to look up at the billowing clouds.

Her mom had followed her. 'Take a jacket,' she said, gazing with concern at Kirstie's troubled grey eyes. 'And don't stay out long.'

Nodding, Kirstie slung the jacket loosely around her shoulders and stepped down into the yard. Shivering, she made a beeline for the tack-room, where she picked up a curry comb and brush, then hurried on across the empty corral to the barn.

The big wooden door creaked on its hinges as she opened it, and a warm, sweet aroma greeted her.

Hay and horses. For Kirstie, not even the most expensive designer perfume could beat that smell. Combined with dust, old leather and the faint suggestion of bitumen paint, the atmosphere in the barn soothed and calmed her, so that she approached the nearest of the stalls in a more composed frame of mind.

'Hey, Yukon,' she murmured, slipping through the wooden gate and running her hand down the paint mare's neck. Then she reached out to pet little Butterscotch.

Both mother and foal snickered in a pleased fashion, rustling the straw under their feet as they shuffled and enjoyed the attention.

Then Kirstie set to with brush and comb, working the dried mud from Yukon's coat, checking every inch of her body to confirm that the flood had done her no lasting harm. After ten minutes' hard brushing, she stepped back, satisfied.

Next in line came Taco and Gulliver, and Kirstie went through the same procedure as before. The mare seemed especially protective of her foal, scarcely letting Kirstie near him, and enduring her own grooming session with bad grace.

'Hey!' Kirstie protested, as a strong head butt sent her staggering back against the partition. 'What happened to your stable manners?'

A newly-brushed Taco snorted to let Kirstie know that it would be best for her to retreat and leave them in peace for a while, which she did.

Then she moved on to Golden Dawn's stall, preparing herself to face the fact that there would be no sweet sorrel foal to pet and fuss.

Goldie stood alone, the picture of misery. Her glorious chestnut coat was dull, her white socks caked in mud. But it was in her eyes that Kirstie saw the worst suffering. Normally shiny and alert, they were now hooded and gave off an impression of confusion and pain. Her head hung low, her whole posture slumped in an attitude of despair.

'I know, I know!' Kirstie breathed, hardly able to bear moving inside that circle of distress. But she did manage at last to reach out and softly stroke Golden Dawn's cheek. 'No, really I don't know in my heart how it feels to lose the most precious thing on earth and realise that he's never coming back. How could I?'

Sighing, Goldie lowered her head still further. She tolerated Kirstie's caress without seeming to notice.

'When my dad left us, way back when we lived in Denver, it was tough,' she went on. 'But at least I knew he was still alive and I could go visit. Losing Tatum is ten times worse than that.'

Golden Dawn's eyelids slowly shut then gradually opened again. It was like all the spirit had gone out of her when she lost her foal and all that was left was a shell.

'. . . Kirstie?' Sandy's footsteps approached down the central aisle of the barn and her voice broke the silence.

Kirstie turned and greeted her with a tear-stained face. 'Mom, I can't bear it!'

'Come back inside,' her mother said gently.

'It's too sad!'

'I know it, but come away. Staying out here doesn't help.' Quietly but firmly, Sandy put an arm around Kirstie's shoulder and took her out of the stall towards the barn door, where she turned off the light and led her slowly away.

7

'Kirstie, how can we ever thank you enough?' was Bonnie Goodman's message.

She'd driven out to the ranch and rushed into the house on a wave of gratitude, hugging everyone in sight, but mostly her red-faced daughter.

'Quit it, Mom!' Lisa had begged, wriggling free and retreating to stand next to Kirstie. The pained expression on her face read 'Mothers! Who needs them?'

'But we owe Kirstie one big, big favour!' Always

tending to go over the top, the recent crisis had sent Bonnie into overdrive. She said she'd driven like a maniac and picked up a speeding ticket for her pains. ('Dumb cop. I told him I had a daughter almost drowned! But did he pay me any mind? No, sir!') She'd even left her End of Trail Diner unattended. ('What was I supposed to do? Stay and cook eggs easy-over with my little girl standing at death's door?')

'Mom, I'm OK!' Lisa had insisted, the colour rising to her cheeks.

'I even had important customers at the time you called.' Bonnie had run on regardless, sitting herself down at the table and accepting a cup of coffee from Sandy. 'Waddie Newton was in town to meet up with a guy from Denver who's interested in buying Aspen Park. But I said, "Waddie, you have to excuse me for shutting up shop on you. My daughter's in trouble. I gotta go." '

The information took Matt off on to a new subject, leaving Lisa and Kirstie to catch their breaths.

'So the land sale looks like a sure thing,' Matt said quietly with a worried frown.

Bonnie nodded and gave him the low-down on the prospective buyer: his height, his weight, the brand of jeans he was wearing. 'His stetson was one hundred per cent beaver,' she assured them. 'That was five hundred dollars worth of hat, believe me!'

'We could do without the Aspen Park problem right now,' Sandy confided. 'We haven't even begun to count the cost of the damage in Pond Meadow, but I know for a fact that most of the fences are down. That's gonna cost plenty for starters. But that's just the tip of the iceberg. The flash flood wrecked the footbridge and tipped a heap of garbage on the banks of Red Fox Meadow too. Luckily, the water level in there didn't rise high enough to endanger the horses . . .'

'Thank God!' Matt cut in. His dark brown eyes had practically vanished behind the frown as he too took stock. 'My beef is that we didn't get any warning from the guys up at Dorfmann.'

'We never do,' Sandy reminded him. 'They reckon it's down to us ranchers to keep up to speed with stuff at the dam, and normally that's part of our routine – a weekly call to the engineers to check out what's going on up there.'

'Thank goodness Hadley's not around to hear that!' Kirstie whispered to Lisa. In fact, come to think of it, she'd not seen the old man since Charlie's last-minute news about the overspill had come through.

'Matt, I've been thinking.' Sandy set her jaw in a resigned manner and spoke low and slow. 'Y'know this conference delegation due to join us first thing tomorrow?'

He nodded, guessing what was coming next.

'It's fifteen US Capital Bank managers from all over the state, out here for their training exercises. Riding horses in the Rockies makes them feel they all belong to the same team. Apparently, adversity brings out the best in them and makes them work together better.' She explained the theory to Bonnie. 'They should've been here a couple of hours back to experience real adversity! Anyways, we're trying to grow the corporate business side of things on the ranch. Only, as it turns out, I reckon we need to cancel our bank managers this coming week.'

'Do we have to?' Matt, who was in charge of making the financial spreadsheets work out, saw the dollars draining away with the aftermath of the flood.

For a while, his business brain came into conflict with Sandy's commonsense, practical view of things, allowing Kirstie and Lisa to slip quietly out of the house.

'More rain!' Lisa sighed, gazing out at a hard, cold sheet of the stuff. It formed puddles in the yard and swept in flurries against the red corrugated roof of the tack-room beyond.

'I can't believe Tatum died!' Kirstie spoke what was in her heart, glancing uncertainly at Lisa. 'I mean, drowning is such a horrible way. And the poor little guy was too young to have it happen.'

'Don't!' Lisa closed her eyes and stepped down from the porch into the driving rain.

'Come back. You'll get soaked!'

'I don't care. It's all my fault.' She walked blindly on.

So Kirstie ran after her, catching hold of her arm and dragging her towards the shelter of the tack-room porch. 'Listen, you wanna know what we should do now?'

'Give up, like you said. Go home. Go to bed.'

The hot tears welled up again and mingled with the cold rain.

'No, idiot! I mean the exact opposite!'

Lisa frowned and shot her a glance. '*Not* give up?'

'You got it! Look, we're all moping around supposin' Tatum must have died out there. You should see Golden Dawn. I never saw a horse so miserable!'

'Don't!' Lisa whispered again. This was an angle she couldn't bear even to imagine.

'No, listen. We're thinking, no way would the foal have swum clear. When what we *should* be doing is checking it out!' As she spoke and partly convinced herself of what she was saying, Kirstie's eyes began to grow wider. 'As a matter of fact, I can't believe we didn't think of it before!'

'Check it out how?' Finding herself backed into the tack-room by Kirstie's eagerness, Lisa bumped into the saddle rack behind her.

'How about we ride out to Pond Meadow and take a look around?' Without waiting for an answer, Kirstie heaved her own saddle off the rack. The heavy stirrups swung with a hollow clunk against the wooden wall.

'In the rain?' Lisa's reluctance found voice in a wimpish complaint.

'Sure, in the rain. Grab a slicker from the hook over there. What are you waiting for?'

Lisa stared back open-mouthed. 'You sure changed your mind!' she pointed out. 'Back there in the house, you were the one who was so certain that no way could Tatum have survived.'

'Forget that. That was me still in trauma. I feel better now. And I think we owe it to both Tatum and Golden Dawn to do this!'

'But is it right?' Forced into action by Kirstie, Lisa slipped her arms into the sleeves of a stiff yellow raincoat. 'What if . . . ?' She hesitated on the brink of stating her worst fear.

'What if we find Tatum's body washed up on the bank after all?' Kirstie said it for her. 'Then at least we know the answer. Whereas, if we don't go out and look for him, there'll always be a huge question mark hanging over us.'

Slowly Lisa nodded. She set her mind on finding a saddle and following Kirstie across the corral to the barn.

Staggering under the heavy weights, with the long yellow slickers flapping against their legs, they trudged through the rain into the dry, warm space where the three mares and two foals were stalled.

'Who are we gonna ride?' Lisa asked, still nervous about the whole thing.

'You could take Yukon,' Kirstie suggested, remembering that the sturdy paint horse had seemed to appreciate the care that had been lavished on her earlier. 'That should work. I'll ride Golden Dawn, because if anyone's tuned in to tracking down Tatum, she's definitely the one!'

Muttering and fumbling, Lisa went into Yukon's stall to saddle her up. 'Who says we're nuts?' she grumbled, setting the saddle square on the mare's back. 'We're only riding out in the pouring rain to a place where we almost drowned, that's all! No problem. So quit complaining, you hear? Just stand easy and let me tighten your cinch, OK?'

All the while Lisa mumbled to her horse, Kirstie worked to get Golden Dawn ready. The sorrel mare was still listless when she entered her stall, but interest flickered in her dull eyes as soon as she saw the saddle. Her silky brown ears pricked up and she twisted her head round to pay attention to the saddle blanket being slung over her back, followed by the solid weight of the saddle itself.

'Did you guess what's about to happen?' Kirstie said lightly, making sure not to startle Goldie when she offered her the bit and bridle. 'That's a good girl. Hold your head nice and steady. Let me buckle this cheek-strap, then you'll be good and ready to go looking for Tatum.'

Preparing to lead their horses out of the barn at the same time, Lisa met up with Kirstie in the central aisle and risked a small grin. 'Listen to us! Anyone would think these mares could understand every word we say!'

Kirstie grinned back. 'Yeah!' she insisted. 'Like; sure they can. They're smarter than the average human, remember!'

'Aren't we gonna tell someone what we're planning?' Lisa remarked as Kirstie reached the corral first and hoisted herself into the saddle.

'And have them write us off as completely crazy?' The casual joke against themselves made them both laugh out loud.

'Kirstie Scott, you're weird, you know that?'

'Sure.' Weird, as in really caring about horses. As in preferring them in many ways to people.

Well, if that was the case, it was OK by her.

Revisiting the scene of the recent flood in Pond Meadow was tough for everyone, as the evidence of its destruction lay all around.

The once peaceful, flower-strewn pasture was now a sea of mud. Limbs of trees and boulders lay stranded a full fifty yards from the creek, while the sturdy footbridge had been broken up and completely washed away.

'How do we cross the creek?' Lisa wanted to know, as Kirstie rode Golden Dawn ahead towards the place where the bridge used to be.

'Like this.' Kirstie urged Golden Dawn to step down into the water, sensing her unease.

The mare's ears were laid flat, and as Kirstie pushed her forwards, she fought for control of her head.

'Take your time. I don't blame you for not wanting to do this. It looks kinda murky, I know. But the water level's back down, see. And if we don't cross, we have no chance of finding out what happened to Tatum.' Easing her patiently into the creek, Kirstie's heart jerked as Golden Dawn missed her footing and stumbled.

But the horse seemed to have understood the object of the exercise and overcame her own natural fear of the swirling brown water. She regained her balance and waded on, staying steady as the level rose almost to her belly.

Seeing Goldie take the lead, plucky Yukon decided to follow. Lisa got her across to the far bank with much less trouble than Kirstie had experienced. 'Now what?' she asked.

'First we locate the last place anyone saw Tatum.' Clear thinking was needed to keep feelings under control, Kirstie knew. 'If the bridge was right here, then the foal was over in this direction, round about this spot.'

Stepping slowly through the oozing mud, Golden Dawn was fully alert. She raised her head to gaze up at the wooded hillside, as if paying close attention to the possibility that her foal had at least had the sense to get up from his knees and flee from the flood in the direction of higher ground.

Who knows, perhaps Goldie even saw that happen, Kirstie thought to herself. *The rest of us were too busy with the other horses and trying to rescue Lisa, but a mother's instinct in a crisis would surely be to follow her foal's every movement.*

'My idea is, we trust Golden Dawn to show us what to do next.' Kirstie shared her theory with Lisa. 'No way will we find any prints down in the meadow because of all this slime and mud and stuff. But if we go up beyond where the water level reached and let Goldie poke around, maybe there'll be a sign which we could pick up and follow.'

'Supposing we can make it.' Lisa pointed out how difficult it was for Yukon and Golden Dawn to make progress across the waterlogged meadow. Their hooves sank deep into the mud and sucked out again as they lifted their feet, so that they were soon breathing hard and working up a sweat. Steam rose from their withers as the rain continued to pelt down.

Patiently Kirstie guided Golden Dawn towards firmer ground. Somehow she could pick up the mare's extra eagerness, despite the heavy going, and she wondered with rising excitement what Goldie might be listening and looking for with her supersensitive ears and eyes.

'Don't you think we'd have spotted Tatum if he'd made it this far?' Beyond the pond, approaching the hillside, Lisa seemed determined not to raise her hopes.

'So why is Goldie so supercharged?' Kirstie asked.

'I didn't know she was.'

'Sure. Look at the angle of her head. What's that if it's not her picking up some pretty hopeful clues?'

'Such as?' Lisa shook her head, showering waterdrops from the peak of her baseball cap. Yukon staggered in the mud and gave a weary snort.

'Well, I can't tell you that. I'm not a horse, am I? But you can bet your life that she's heard or seen something good.'

Lisa said she'd believe that when she bumped right into it. 'Honest, Kirstie, I don't want to give you an argument here. But really, you shouldn't get your hopes up just yet.'

For a while they went on in silence, Kirstie resenting Lisa's negative attitude, Lisa sitting in the saddle, shoulders hunched. Giving Golden Dawn her head, Kirstie found that they crept up slowly between the trees more or less taking the route chosen by the bear only the night before.

And she could see what a difference twelve hours had made to the wildlife of the area. Whereas before the flood there would scarcely have been any sign of the small nocturnal creatures of the wood, now the place was a hive of activity. She saw a family of raccoons – mother and four babies – hastily scraping out a den in the base of a hollow tree. The chunky adult bustled through the wet undergrowth carrying leaves and grass to line the new home, her ringed tail trailing, the black markings like a mask around her eyes giving her a worried, fugitive look.

Further along the trail, Lisa squealed and Yukon skittered sideways at an irate skunk arching her back and stamping her front feet at them from the safety of a mossy log. Later still, Kirstie picked up probable signs of bobcats in the area: a dead rat, red and raw, splayed out beside a rocky crevice, heavy feline paw prints sunk deep into the mud nearby.

And still the rain came down without relief, filling the narrow mountain creeks to overflowing, making them bubble and spurt over rocks and across the trail.

When they came within sight of the towering cliffs of Miners' Ridge and heard the swollen waterfall tumbling into the deep pool at the end of the culvert, Lisa reined her horse to a halt. 'Honest to God, Kirstie, I don't believe Yukon can go much further!'

Forging ahead with Golden Dawn, Kirstie didn't want to stop. But she glanced back to see that the paint horse was blowing badly. Her head hung low and her brown-and-white sides heaved in and out as they faced yet another steep incline.

'OK, why don't you two stop and take a rest?' she suggested. 'Goldie wants to keep right on going, so we'll take a look through Dead Man's Canyon and along the ridge. When Yukon's got her breath back you could cut out the ridge and head directly upstream to Marshy Meadows. We'll meet you down there in thirty minutes.'

Glad to agree, Lisa sat tight under a tree while Kirstie and Golden Dawn made their way towards a narrow channel called Fat Man's Squeeze. Rain spattered with extra force as the wind shook the trees and sent the drops cascading down. Deep in the twenty foot high Squeeze, Kirstie came across more remains. This time it was a rabbit who had met a sudden and violent end, probably at the hands of a coyote, to judge by the sharp claw marks and lighter prints.

Shuddering, Kirstie made Goldie tread carefully over the stringy, rain soaked carcass, and was glad when they emerged into the basin of Dead Man's Canyon, where Golden Dawn insisted on stopping dead in her tracks.

'What is it?' Kirstie looked and listened. But the roar of the waterfall filled her head. 'Enough water!' she said out loud, reining Goldie to the right to take the steep slope on to the ridge.

But the sorrel mare refused to move. Even when Kirstie dug in her heels and shifted her weight, she stood with feet planted, quivering slightly.

'Hey!' Kirstie stopped kicking and sat very still. Was this where Tatum had scrambled for refuge after escaping the terrifying flood? Maybe, just maybe . . .

Golden Dawn pricked her ears and flared her nostrils. Her tail went tight against her rump.

'What did you see?' Kirstie peered through the sheet of rain down the length of the narrow canyon. It was understandable that Goldie's mood was fearful, after all she'd been through.

The rain rattled down through the pine canopy overhead, falling on to small, slender aspen boughs and shaking the leaves of thorn bushes beneath.

'Don't you like it here?' Kirstie murmured, ready to let her horse retreat.

Goldie quivered. Small muscles jumped down the length of her back; her eyes stared wide.

And then, at last, Kirstie saw what was wrong.

There was a huge, sandy-coloured creature staring down from a rock. The giant cat had startling amber eyes outlined in black like an Egyptian goddess. Her muzzle was white and soft, her wide paws planted firmly as she crouched and kept them in her sights.

'Mountain lion!' Kirstie whispered.

Big; very big . . . maybe eight feet long. Strong.

Golden Dawn stood paralysed, head averted, staring wildly out of the corner of her vision.

And the hungry lion shuffled forward to the edge of her rock, ready to pounce.

8

A seriously scared horse will freeze. Kirstie knew this and felt Golden Dawn tighten up until she stood rigid.

The lion crept on, beautiful and deadly. Her golden eyes blazed, she crouched low, every muscle ready for action.

Kirstie sat mesmerised. Never in all her years on the ranch had she come across this most elusive of forest creatures, and strangely, despite the danger, she was enthralled.

The bright, fiery gaze . . . the perfect balance.

Nearer still, poised on the edge of the rock.

At the final moment, Golden Dawn came back to life. With Kirstie firm in the saddle, she raised herself on to her hind legs and struck out at the crouching lion.

Then, *crash!* A rifle shot split the silence.

The bullet smashed through the leaves and hit the rock above the lion's head.

The big cat recoiled and leaped back close in against an overhang. She opened her mouth in a wide snarl, fangs bared.

Crash! A second shot ricocheted through the trees with a piercing whine.

'Oh God, oh God!' Kirstie gasped as Golden Dawn writhed in mid-air and landed off-balance. For a split second she thought her horse had been hit and wounded.

Above their heads, the mountain lion cowered in the shadows, waiting to see if a third shot came her way. Hidden birds started and rose raucously from the trees, flapping skywards.

Disbelieving, Kirstie froze in confusion. Who was firing the gun?

Up on the ridge, an empty cartridge fell to the

ground, and there was the metal click of a new one being loaded.

But before the shot could be fired, as the gunman levelled the long barrel and took aim, the lion recovered her wits. With a vicious snarl she charged out from the overhang and, in one smooth movement, sprang out above the place where Kirstie and Golden Dawn stood.

Kirstie saw the blurred image, the white underbelly, before she closed her eyes tight shut and prayed.

When she opened them again, the lion had leaped clean over them and landed on a rock to their right. Her legs absorbed the shock of landing, straightened and jumped a second time, springing up the scaly bark of a pine tree, clinging with lethal claws and hauling herself out of sight.

Terrified, Golden Dawn whirled round on the spot, her flight mechanism kicking in at last. Kirstie held her still with all her might. 'Easy!' she gasped. 'Whoa!' No way did she want to risk blundering through the undergrowth with a maniac marksman still pointing a rifle in their direction.

A figure emerged high on Miners' Ridge.

Wearing a beaten-up stetson and a long slicker, casually carrying a rifle under his arm, he began to make his way down into the canyon.

'You could've got us killed!' Kirstie yelled, anger bubbling up into her throat. 'Are you crazy? You pointed that thing right at us!'

The tall, thin man didn't reply but kept on coming.

'Call yourself a gunman? Why, I bet you never even learned to shoot proper! I'm telling you, with a target as big as that lion, any fool hunter could've hit it!' Beside herself, and still fighting to control Golden Dawn, Kirstie let rip with the first insults that came into her head.

'I wasn't aiming to kill the crittur. Scarin' her off was all.'

'Huh?' Finally Kirstie regained control of her frightened horse. There was something about the slow, gravelly voice that was familiar. And she thought she recognised the slight stoop of the shoulders, the lean jaw under that rain-darkened white stetson.

'I said, I wasn't shootin' to kill. Only to send her runnin'.'

'Hadley!' Kirstie yelped as the man reached the

bottom of the canyon and tipped back the brim of his hat to reveal his face. 'Jeez, you just gave us the fright of our lives!'

'It's like this.' Hadley took his time with the explanations as usual. 'I'm the one caused this problem, so I'm the one to put it right.'

Before giving his reasons for being there, he'd made Kirstie wait. First there was his mount, Crazy Horse, to retrieve from the hidden draw by Fat Man's Squeeze, his rifle to strap on to the saddle-bag, then five minutes to double-check that the lion had been scared off good and proper.

'I knew I hadn't seen you since the flood,' Kirstie realised. 'But I guess I thought you'd gone and buried your head in your cabin.'

The old man gave her a level stare. 'Like I said, this is my problem. A man's gotta own up to his responsibilities, don't he?'

'Yes but no one thinks you're to blame!' Dismounting from her horse, Kirstie found that her legs were shaking and her fingers hardly able to hang on to the reins.

'I shoulda made that call like the boss told me,' he said stubbornly. 'Then we'd have moved those mares and foals out of Pond Meadow, knowing that Dorfmann was due to release overspill. All this is down to me.'

'And when did you ride Crazy Horse out?'

'Just before the flood hit. I reckoned I could pull the mares and foals out of the meadow up on to the hill by knocking down a couple of fence posts and leading them away from the creek. So I saddled up and packed my rifle just in case. Only I didn't have time to act. That wall of water beat me to it.'

'Likewise.' Kirstie had a flash of action replay: the wave crashing through the rocky channel, curling over their heads. 'But if you were up on high ground, you must've seen exactly what happened!'

'Pretty much,' Hadley admitted. 'I saw you get five of the horses out, and I saw the sorrel foal get left behind.'

'And what then?' She could hardly force the all important question out, she was so afraid of what the answer might be.

'His luck was in,' Hadley said in his slow, even voice. 'He got caught up in the flood and it carried him out across the pond. He went under a couple of times, but a foal knows how to swim if need be. And the current wasn't too strong that far from the creek. In the end he managed to pull himself clear.'

Kirstie stared at Hadley until she could piece together the message he was giving her. 'Tatum's alive?' she stuttered.

'I'm not sayin' that.' He stemmed her eagerness by holding up both hands. 'All I'm sayin' is, the flood never claimed him. And I'm hopin'.'

'So he *is* alive!' What else could this mean?

Hadley gave it to her straight. 'Listen. The foal makes it through the water. But Crazy Horse don't like what's happenin' in the meadow: trees torn up, water flowin' in where it don't belong. So he starts actin' up pretty bad. It takes all my ability to stay in the saddle, and by the time I get to look for Tatum again, why he ain't nowhere around!'

'He ran off?' *Alive, but on the run!* Just wait until she got hold of Lisa and told her!

Hadley shrugged. 'Maybe. I've been out lookin' for him ever since, but I ain't seen hide nor hair.'

'But that's because the rain washed away all his tracks!'

'Or because somethin' else moved in on him. Coyote, mountain lion . . .' Hadley's expression and characteristic shrug said it all

Yeah, there was that. In all this natural upheaval, with every nocturnal creature on the move in broad daylight, the dangers to a weak, two month foal multiplied like crazy. Kirstie's shoulders sagged and her gaze fell to the sodden forest floor.

'Come nightfall, we get more trouble.' Hadley fiddled edgily with Crazy Horse's cinch strap. 'I hear the temperature's set for ten below freezing. If this rain turns to snow, I don't give much for Tatum's chances of makin' it through to daybreak.'

'So let's go!' Obviously this was no time to stand here discussing the pros and cons. The facts were these – Tatum had survived the flood, they had four hours before dusk, and there was a whole lot of territory to cover.

As they rode out through the Squeeze and put Golden Dawn and Crazy Horse into a trot towards Marshy Meadows, Kirstie filled Hadley in on the plan to meet Lisa. 'Did you look for Tatum there yet?' she asked.

'Nope. I didn't get that far up-river.'

'Well, let's hope Lisa found something.' During the fifteen minute ride, Kirstie kept this thought to the front of her mind.

And when they crested the ridge and dipped down in to the basin of the meadow where the cattle had grazed, she saw her friend immediately raise her arm in greeting and lope up the hill to meet them.

'Hey, Hadley!' Lisa greeted the old man hurriedly without stopping to wonder what the heck he was doing there. She reined Yukon to a halt and poured out her news to Kirstie without even pausing for breath. 'What kept you? I've been waiting hours! You gotta come this way and see what I found! There's fresh poop not far from Deadwood Cemetery. Only Deadwood Cemetery got washed away by the flood, so it ain't there no more. Fresh *horse* poop, not cattle, not deer . . . D'you hear me? A horse has been in the meadow since the flash flood. That can only mean Tatum . . .'

Kirstie and Hadley got the gist and gave each other a businesslike nod. All three turned their horses ready for a cavalry charge along the length of Marshy Meadows.

'Yee-hah!' Kirstie cried as Golden Dawn galloped ahead. She ducked under tree branches and swerved around bends, while the horse splashed through puddles at breakneck speed as though her life depended on it.

She knows! Kirstie thought. *This mare can sense her foal is down here somewhere! We're getting there, Tatum! Hang on!*

The sorrel mare loped flat out, straining through the bit, head forward and mane flying, hooves pounding down the soft dirt track.

She only halted when she reached the site that had until recently been Deadwood Cemetery.

'Jeez!' Kirstie said as Goldie pulled up short. The high wall of branches and logs, jammed between two tall rocks, that had built up over successive floods had caved in completely. Debris was scattered far and wide: gnarled trunks, decaying branches, even whole root clusters with their twisted, blackened, dripping fingers.

'Yeah, I know!' Lisa was next to arrive at the scene of devastation. 'Imagine that!'

'That's years of build-up all smashed away in a

second.' Kirstie pictured the explosive force of the Dorfmann overspill. And then she noticed a surprising feature of the rearranged, sodden landscape. 'Say, there's a narrow draw off to the right, beyond that pointed rock. I never knew it existed!'

'So, play explorer some other time!' Impatient to show Kirstie and Hadley the vital Tatum clue, Lisa reined Yukon to the left, picking her way through the scattered driftwood towards a shallow rise.

Kirstie let Hadley follow, but took into account a strong feeling that Golden Dawn didn't want to go along too. 'What is it?' she murmured, leaning forward in the saddle.

The mare was listening intently to a sound beyond the two rocks. She took a step forward, listened again.

'Kirstie, come see!' Lisa's voice urged from a distance. 'Hadley agrees with me. It's foal droppings for sure!'

Weighing this up, she took the decision to follow Goldie's instinct. 'That's great!' she called back. 'You two take a look over there. I'm gonna try the new culvert!'

That was if her horse could negotiate the clutter of logs and branches still blocking the entrance. Goldie rapped her hooves against the obstacles, stumbled, went determinedly on.

'Maybe I'll walk alongside.' Quickly Kirstie slipped from the saddle and helped by pushing aside some of the debris. She heaved and leaned with all her weight to clear a path, but it was slow work, and Golden Dawn wanted to bruise her way through using brute force. 'Easy!' Kirstie had to insist. 'You'll break a leg if you try to do it that way!'

Warm! A voice at the back of her head kept whispering, as in the old seeking game she'd played when she was a kid. *Warmer! Keep going! You're getting hot . . . hotter . . . boiling!*

In search of her precious foal, Golden Dawn blundered through the last of the driftwood into unknown territory.

No one had trodden in this draw for years, maybe even decades. Thick with tangled undergrowth, dripping in the rain, it seemed to be a natural magnet for whatever mist and cloud was around. 'Goldie?' Kirstie called, reaching out for an insubstantial shape only yards from where she stood.

The horse snickered uneasily, pushing ahead through the thorn bushes whose spikes pierced Kirstie's trousers and stabbed into her flesh. In front of them was a thick curtain of wet grey mist, trapped by the ever-narrowing walls of rock to either side.

'Are you certain about this?' Kirstie murmured to Golden Dawn. It didn't seem to her like a place a lost foal would choose as a refuge. Horses preferred wide open spaces, a chance to flee at danger. This draw was too narrow, shadowed by overhanging rocks, and finishing in a dead-end.

The mare stopped to listen.

Drip-drip-drip. Though the rain was easing, there was water everywhere. It trickled down the black rocks, ran along the bottom of the culvert, dropped from the aspens over their heads.

Then Kirstie heard a sharp, dry sound; the crack of a twig underfoot.

Golden Dawn stiffened. Her ears flicked in the direction of the sound.

'Tatum?'

A second crack, then a rustle of leaves.

Golden Dawn whinnied with a high, nervous whine.

Then a deer sprang out of a crevice in the rock, bursting right on to them, making Kirstie fall backwards into the bushes. Its long legs took it in a sideways dart, a blunder against a tree trunk, another sharp change of direction, eyes wide and dark with fear.

Goldie squealed and reared; the mule deer darted away, hopping, bounding, leaping free of the culvert.

9

'So you made a mistake? It happens.' Disentangling herself from the painful thorn bushes, Kirstie resigned herself to the fact that Golden Dawn's famous maternal sixth sense had for once let her down. She picked up her hat from the mud and jammed it on to her head.

Goldie skittered and pranced, ran smack into a nearby tree, whacked her shoulder, whirled and reared. *Mistake? Me? No way!*

('Kirstie! Where are you? It's me!' Lisa's voice

broke in. It seemed to come from a million miles away.)

'Easy, girl!' Kirstie soothed, trying to grab hold of the reins. 'What you thought was Tatum turned out to be a plain old mule deer. Tough. But it doesn't mean we give up.'

Backing off down the concealed culvert, Golden Dawn resisted all Kirstie's attempts to lead her out.

('Kirstie, answer me! I got a message from Hadley!')

'C'mon, why are you fooling around? This is no time for playing games.' Surprised at how spooked Goldie was by the deer, Kirstie decided to back off. Soon the mare would quieten down and agree to walk out into the open.

So she stood for a few moments and watched her spin round in the enclosed space, loose reins flying, stirrups swinging wide. It was no good; Kirstie would have to take more direct action to get her out.

'OK, so we get tough.' Cornering her against a boulder, Kirstie managed to nip nimbly into the saddle. She set her heels against Golden Dawn's flanks and urged her on.

The mare braced her legs and refused to move.

'Let's go!' Kirstie clicked her tongue and kicked a second time.

Goldie tossed her head. With a backwards glance at Kirstie, she sat down on her haunches and smoothly rolled on to her side.

'Hey!' It took a rapid reaction for Kirstie to leap clear in time. 'That was my leg you almost crushed!'

Free of her rider and covered in grey mud, Golden Dawn struggled to her feet and moved further down the culvert.

('Can you hear me, Kirstie? Hadley said for me to tell you he reckons there's another flood moving downriver! He went up on to the ridge to take a look!')

'What are you trying to tell me?' Her attention glued to Golden Dawn's antics, Kirstie missed the faint message drifting down from the mouth of the gulley. Ignoring Lisa, she frantically tried to work out what the mare's stubborn disobedience might mean. 'OK, so you won't admit you were wrong. You want us to take a look down the far end of the gulley?'

'Kirstie, I'm coming in after you!' Lisa's

troubled voice broke through the confusion at last. 'If Hadley's right about the water level rising again, we don't have time for hide and seek, OK?'

'No, Lisa, stay where you are. I hear you!' Kirstie spun round to yell her answer. She felt a cold tingle like icy water trickle down her spine.

'You and Golden Dawn have to get the heck out, OK! Hadley's pretty sure the river's swelling up fast. He says it's probably snowmelt combined with this stupid rain!' Lisa's voice broke with anxiety and came out as a scratchy croak.

'OK, OK, I'm doing my best. Goldie's playing up. I'll be out as fast as I can!'

Think about it, she told herself. *If Shady River floods a second time, the water's gonna come pouring over that shelf of rock at the end of the culvert, just like before. It's gonna create one heck of a waterfall and fill up the whole gulley in the next to no time!*

The thought made her gasp and sprint towards Golden Dawn. 'Let's go!' she pleaded, succeeding in catching hold of one rein and tugging the mare's head towards the exit.

Was it sheer badness that made Goldie dig in her heels? Had the day's experiences soured her nature and made her mistrust everything that Kirstie tried to do?

Or was she saying, *No way! My foal's in here somewhere, and I'd give up my own life sooner than leave him!*

Of course! How dumb could you get? In a flash, Kirstie understood that though the deer had proved a false alarm, the mother's instinct was still to be relied on.

'Where is he? Where's Tatum?' Releasing the pressure on the rein, she blundered after Golden Dawn.

('Kirstie, it's true. Hadley's riding down from the ridge. He says to get you out of the draw fast!')

No time to play safe and pick a way through the tangle of overgrown trees. Best to give Goldie free rein, follow her over fallen logs, through the stream that ran ankle-deep at the far end of the gulley. Kirstie splashed up to her knees in her hurry to keep up with the eager horse.

Rocks towered to either side; trees thrust and leaned crazily out of surfaces that offered hardly any soil, closing in a dark arch over their heads. And water came spilling down from the ledge of rock, at first a thin trickle, growing visibly as the seconds ticked by.

'Tatum!' Seized by panic, Kirstie sobbed out the lost foal's name.

And the mother raised her own voice in a shrill whinny which was deadened by the walls of rock and by the splash and crash of water.

They'd reached the end. The cliffs had narrowed to a full-stop, cold water rained down on them without mercy.

At the edge of a swiftly rising pool, Golden Dawn turned and looked helplessly into Kirstie's eyes. *Where now?*

Suppose I was lost. Suppose I'd gone through all this, only to find myself trapped in a place I'd never been before. I'd be scared and confused. All I'd want in the whole world would be to be with my mom! 'Let's call again!' she whispered to Golden Dawn. 'Make it loud. Pray that he hears us!'

Together they filled their lungs with air and cried out.

And this time there was an answer.

Faint and weak. Unmistakeable.

Golden Dawn plunged across the icy pool towards a shallow cave – the only dry spot around.

The hiss and splash of water created a haze that half hid the horse from Kirstie's view, until she too plunged into the pool and followed.

There on a ledge inside the cave, Tatum lay. A dark, spindly shape, almost black, with the strong white flash on his forehead. The marking was what helped Kirstie pick him out amongst the brushwood and straggly bushes.

She watched Goldie approach the shivering bundle and reach her head into the cave. Mother nudged at her baby with urgent little movements. *How bad is it? Can you stand? Come on, we need to get out of here!*

Tatum raised his heavy head, his eyelids drooping; he had no energy to move from his chosen refuge.

So Kirstie moved in. She climbed on to the slippery ledge and eased both arms under the dazed foal. When she picked him up, he seemed light – almost skin and bone.

Gently she carried him down from the cave and across the rising pool. The water reached past her knees, overflowed the pool and formed a fresh channel down the middle of the culvert.

And gradually, from feeling like a

featherweight, head lolling, limbs drooping, he grew heavy in Kirstie's arms. The draw was a hundred yards long. After twenty, she staggered. At thirty, she had to put Tatum down and rest.

('Kirstie, where are you? For God's sakes, answer me!')

Crouching on the ground to catch her breath, Kirstie felt Golden Dawn push at her from behind. *Don't stop! No time! Keep moving!*

'Yeah!' Kirstie seized at a new idea. Why not lift Tatum and lay him across his mother's back? She needed enough strength to lift him and arrange him steadily, enough time to do the deed before the flood overtook them.

Golden Dawn stood firm and took Tatum's weight. Then she plunged on towards the outlet.

They emerged in the nick of time, out of the shadows into the grey mist of the easing rain.

Hadley was there, approaching them on foot, taking Goldie's reins and steadying the exhausted foal. And Lisa ran to fling both arms around Kirstie as, for the second time that day, they cheated the force of nature and survived the flood.

* * *

'Lucky!' Matt expressed the commonsense view of the day's events.

'Luck had nothing to do with it,' Lisa insisted. 'It was pure skill and savvy.'

'Horse savvy,' Kirstie agreed. She described over and over how Golden Dawn had never given up on finding Tatum alive, how some invisible radar built into Goldie's brain had told her exactly where to look.

The rescue party had climbed out of Marshy Meadow only minutes ahead of the overspill from Shady River filling up the hidden culvert and bursting out through the old Deadwood Cemetery into the green pasture. Shaking, counting their blessings, yet cursing the rain, they'd slowly made their way back to the ranch.

And they'd been greeted by a worried group preparing to set up a search party of their own once they discovered that three horses and three riders had gone missing in the afternoon downpour.

'Did I get this right?' Sandy had insisted on Kirstie repeating the story. 'Since you left here two hours back, you've been attacked by a mountain lion, shot at, got trapped in a place no one knew existed, and half-drowned for a second time in one day?'

Kirstie had nodded; every word was true. 'But Golden Dawn found Tatum!' she insisted. The proof was right here in the barn, settled down in the thickest, warmest bed of hay. He'd been rubbed down, fed, watered and was now sleeping peacefully while his mother tucked into the biggest bucket of grain . . .

'And Hadley gave early warning of the second flood,' Lisa reminded everyone. She didn't want the old wrangler's part to be forgotten.

'Not to mention saving me and Goldie from the lion!' Kirstie added.

'Talk about redeeming your past mistakes!' Matt murmured.

Of course, when they looked around to thank him, Hadley's yellow slicker and hat were hanging on his hook, but there was no sign of the man himself.

Later, after Matt had given both Golden Dawn and Tatum a thorough veterinary check and pronounced them both fit after their ordeal, Bonnie Goodman drove Lisa home.

'Next time I send my daughter out here for a weekend's leisure riding, remind me to give her swimming instruction and provide her with a life-jacket!' Bonnie quipped at Sandy.

Lisa had grinned at Kirstie. *Mothers!*

And there was even a follow-on after supper that evening, when the phone rang and Kirstie picked up the call.

'Get this!' Lisa gushed. 'You know Waddie Newton was in here earlier with the guy who planned to buy Aspen Park? Well, here's some good news. Mr Developer-from-Denver hears everyone in town discussing the flash flood. He makes a few inquiries, finds out that Dorfmann dumps its overspill at least twice annually, decides that no way is he gonna invest in expensive real estate that's liable to vanish under water a couple of times a year–'

'The deal's off!' Kirstie cut in. 'Wow, wait till I tell my mom!'

'So every cloud has a silver lining,' Sandy said when she heard the news. 'That's what they always say. And in this case it happens to be literally true!'

'Until next time Waddie Newton gets an offer he can't refuse,' Matt added quietly.

Kirstie pummelled him with a cushion, then went out to check one last time on Golden Dawn and her foal.

Warm, sweet darkness. Hay-sweet. Barn-dark.

Horses breathing.

Kirstie stepped softly down the aisle, heart beating slow, filling her lungs with the contented air.

Yukon and Butterscotch stood in the first stall munching hay. Gulliver and Taco nosed in the framework of the second door as she passed by to reach Goldie and Tatum.

Her figure cast a long, fuzzy shadow in the dim glow of a far-off bulb; enough light to see that mare and foal were content.

More than content, Kirstie felt. Relieved and glad to be home. Proud.

She read it in Golden Dawn's arched neck, in the shine of her eye as she lowered her head to nuzzle her shiny sorrel son. *We made it. It didn't look like we would, but trust me; when we hear the word 'quit', we don't even know what it means!*